A Kidnapped Collie

THE REBECCA ORANGE CASTLE COZY MYSTERY SERIES
BOOK FOUR

VALERIE BRANDY

Published by: Emerald Lion Press. 23901 Calabasas Rd., Ste 2088, Calabasas, CA 91302. emeraldlionpress@gmail.com

ISBN: 978-1-964161-63-1

Editing provided by Sharon Lennon-Mehlschau.

Printed in the United States of America. To request permission to use passages from this book in any context other than a review, please contact the publisher at emeraldlionpress@gmail.com.

Visit the author's website at: www.valeriebrandy.com

✷ Formatted with Vellum

Contents

CHAPTER

One

"I WANT what you Americans would call a *'mutt,'*" Jack says, smiling at me. We're standing in front of a three-story stone building painted a soft peachy-pink. Worn wooden trim circles the windows. A hand-carved wooden sign that reads *"Atwood Animal Rescue"* hangs above the door, swinging gently in the spring breeze. "I'm looking for a dog with a scrappy spirit. Someone who hasn't had it easy in life, but has continued to show up and do his best anyway."

"Why do you assume this dog is *'he'*?" I say playfully, nudging Jack in the ribs. "Plenty of us women out there are scrappy. I think I'm Exhibit A."

"You're quite right," Jack nods seriously. "Tenacity is a feature I quite admire in a woman. That much is clear. Shall we go find my new companion?" Jack walks toward the building, looking nervous. "Oh goodness, what if she doesn't like me? I'll be a Duke with a dog that hates him."

"You haven't even met her yet and you're already catastrophizing," I cluck. Beside me, Joe wags his tail and offers a helpful bark of agreement. "Joe says he can't imagine a dog not liking you," I add, translating for him.

"I hope he's right," Jack says. "This building used to be

the old village post office," he explains as he pushes open the heavy wooden door. "If you haven't noticed by now, Monrovians enjoy repurposing old buildings for new purposes."

The interior of the space is the most welcoming animal shelter I've ever been in. Where American animal shelters prioritize cement and cages, this place feels like someone's beloved country home that happens to house rescue animals. Gleaming hardwood floors stretch across the reception area. The walls, painted the same soft peach as the exterior, display framed photos of successfully adopted pets with their new families.

"They renovated about two years ago," Jack continues, leading me past the front desk where a young woman greets him with a mix of warmth and distance. It's clear she recognizes Jack, but doesn't want to make a fuss. This is something I've been getting used to while dating Jack— the fact that he's a Duke makes interactions with strangers incredibly… awkward.

"Your Grace," the woman says, standing. "My goodness— we weren't— no one alerted us you were coming by. We would have picked up the place…"

"Last-minute decision," Jack responds with an easy smile. "I'm here with an animal expert, Miss—"

"Miss Orange!" The woman says, appearing almost as excited to see me as she is to see Jack. "I've seen your Royal Investigators office near the village square. And I recognize you from the magazine covers. You look so much better in person."

Thanks, I think, trying to keep from rolling my eyes. *Glad to know I'm not as hideous in real life as I am on the cover of a magazine that's read by millions.*

The woman bends down to Joe and scratches him behind his ears. "And this must be the dog from the photo! Oh, he's *très magnifique.*"

"Rebecca and Joe are here to help me pick out a new companion," the Duke says.

"A Royal pet? We're honored!" the woman says. "Feel free to explore," she tells us. "The dogs are on the first floor, cats and reptiles upstairs. I'm Marie. You can call my name if you need anything." Then, she pauses hopefully, "Or, I could give you a tour if you'd like? Tell you about each of the animals?"

"That would be wonderful," Jack confirms. "We're looking for a dog, so we can politely skip the lizards." His hand finds mine again as we move toward a hallway lined with rooms rather than cages. Each has a glass front and a wooden door, making the space feel more like a pet hotel than a shelter. Inside every room is a comfortable-looking bed, toys, and in most cases, a hopeful furry face.

"The village designed it so the dogs wouldn't feel confined," Marie explains, her voice dropping to a reverent hush as we approach the first room.

"It's wonderful that each dog gets their own space while they're waiting for a *fur*-ever home," Jack says, emphasizing the word "fur."

"Did you just make a word pun?" I tease.

"I did," Jack admits.

Marie stops at an adorable chocolate Labrador with a graying muzzle that thumps his tail against the floor at our approach.

"That's Biscuit," Marie says wistfully. "He's been here about six months. Lovely temperament, but most families want younger dogs I'm afraid. It's not his fault he's an older man. He has so much to offer, if someone would only look deeper at who he really is."

I kneel down to be at eye level with Biscuit, who presses his nose to the glass. "Senior dogs are underrated," I say. "Labs can live fifteen years or more with proper care. His best years are ahead of him! And he's past the destructive chewing phase, which is a bonus."

Jack looks at me with undisguised admiration. "You can tell all that just by looking at him?"

I laugh. "Twenty-three years at the Safari Park, and before that, four years of veterinary school and two more specializing in exotic animal behavior. See how his ears are relaxed but attentive? How he's wagging but not jumping? He's well-socialized, confident but not overly excitable."

Jack opens the door, and Biscuit approaches us with dignified enthusiasm. I run my hands along his coat, checking muscle tone and movement.

"He's in excellent health for his age," I confirm. "Someone trained him well before he ended up here."

"His owner passed away," Marie says quietly. "He would just love to find a new home."

We move from room to room, taking in the unique personalities on display. A scrappy terrier batters a puzzle toy with wild determination, and I can't help commenting, "That one needs a job— or he'll find one on your shoes."

Jack laughs and points out a sleek cream-colored dog lying regally in the corner. "And this elegant creature?"

"Saluki mix," I say. "Sensitive and fast. She'll bond hard to the right person."

Marie fills in the backstories as we go— telling us about dogs found wandering, surrendered, inherited from relatives. Each story lands with a quiet weight, but Jack listens to every word, his hand never leaving mine. As we continue, I'm struck by how natural it feels to be choosing a dog with Jack — how *right* it is to be here with him.

We turn a corner and Jack slows, his gaze caught by a quiet room at the end of the hall.

"Who's that?" he asks, already drifting toward the glass.

Inside sits a slender, medium-sized dog with alert ears and watchful eyes. Her white coat glows softly in the sunlight, with golden-brown patches along her face and back.

Unlike the others, she doesn't rush to the front or wag— she simply watches, calm and curious.

"Collie mix," I murmur. "Maybe some Spaniel in there, too."

"She showed up a few weeks ago," Marie says. "No ID. She broke into *Le Petit Scone* and helped herself to Henri's croissants."

Jack chuckles, crouching. "She's audacious. Smart. A survivor." He presses his hand to the glass.

The dog tilts her head, then rises and pads over, placing her nose exactly where Jack's hand rests.

"Anyone who bothers Henri is good in my book," I say, bending down to get a closer look at the dog. "You stole croissants from *Le Petit Scone?* Good girl!"

The dog tilts her head to the side, almost smiling as if I've told her a hilarious joke.

"May we meet her?" he asks without looking away.

Marie opens the door, and we step inside. The dog sits again, calm and waiting. Jack kneels, holding out his hand.

"Hello there," he says softly.

She approaches with quiet confidence, pressing her head beneath his palm. He strokes her gently, and I see the tension ease from both of them.

"She likes you," I say, heart swelling. Some bonds you choose. Others *find* you.

"What's her name?" Jack asks.

"She doesn't have one yet. We've just been calling her the little collie."

Jack scratches behind her ears, then smiles softly. "Luma."

"Luma?" I echo.

"It means 'light.' And look at her—she glows. Besides, I think she'll be a light for me." His eyes flick to mine, and something warm settles in my chest. "What do you think?" he asks. "Would you and Joe approve?"

Before I can answer, Joe bounds over and gives Luma a

giant, unsolicited face kiss. She startles, then playfully tackles him. They tumble into a happy blur of fur and paws.

"I think she fits in just fine," I laugh, kneeling beside them. "She's about six— smart, steady. Definitely a herder. She'll need a job."

"She can help with the goose patrol," Jack says seriously.

I raise an eyebrow. "You mean the three geriatric geese who sunbathe by the lake?"

"Exactly. A high-stakes assignment."

"Or she could supervise Chef Renauld in the kitchen," I joke. "Since she was already such a success as sous-chef at *Le Petit Scone.*"

Jack grins. "I want to adopt her. Today."

Marie reappears with paperwork. "I thought you might," she smiles, passing him the paperwork. People who work at rescues can always tell when a bond has been made.

As Jack fills in his name and address, Luma curls at his feet. He strokes her back absentmindedly, already claiming her as his. And I watch, struck by how telling this moment is —how Jack didn't choose the flashiest or easiest dog. He didn't go for the most beautiful dog, or the most energetic, or even the most affectionate. He chose the one with the most pluck. He chose the survivor, who never gave up on finding her home.

Jack looks up, his gaze traveling down the hallway where we can see other dogs in their rooms. There's guilt in his eyes.

"There are so many of them," he says, his voice tinged with concern. "I just— I feel awful leaving any of them behind."

"I know," I agree, cringing. One of the hardest parts of being an animal trainer is exposure to the suffering of crea-tures you love. And— even though this shelter is beautiful, as far as rescues go— it's not a permanent home. "I wish there were something we could do." Then, it hits me. "Wait a second, Jack. You're a Duke. There *is* something we can do."

"There is?"

"We live on the grounds of a *castle*. I'm already in charge of the menagerie. What's a dozen more dogs?"

"Are you— Rebecca— are you sure you'd be willing to—"

"Of course," I wave a hand. "As long as you don't mind hiring a few more hands—"

"Whatever it takes!" Jack exclaims. "We have several unused outbuildings. The old stable block has twenty stalls that we're not using for horses anymore..."

"They'll roam the grounds," I agree, nodding. "We could even allow staff to adopt a dog if they want one, and that particular dog can stay in that staff member's apartment at night. If you're alright with it, that is—"

"Of *course* I am!"

"And I can offer doggy day care during the day when the staff is working. I'll train them all to work as a pack. Gosh, maybe they can even help me herd the zebras and the sheep. They're always wandering away from the hillside…"

Marie enters again, paperwork in hand. She snaps the top of a brown clipboard, holding a pen. "I'll just need you to—"

"We'll take them all," Jack says brightly.

Marie's mouth drops open. "You— you want— all of them?"

"Every dog here. We'll take them all. They'll live at the castle and help the staff around the grounds." He bends down, brushing his hand over Luma's ear. "But Luma will be the Duke's companion, if that's alright with her."

Luma jumps up and tackles him, making Jack laugh as he falls back onto the floor. It's almost as if she's understood what he's said— like she knows she's finally going home.

After sorting out extensive paperwork with Marie and arranging for Enrique to pick up the rest of the dogs in phases, Jack, Joe, Luma, and I make our way out of the rescue and enjoy a stroll across the village. Jack looks down at Luma, who's walking perfectly on a leash— except for when she insists on stopping to sniff at every street corner.

"Thank you, Rebecca," Jack says as we pause at a small village square with a fountain. "For supporting this idea of taking all the dogs. I know it wasn't what you signed on for when you agreed to manage the castle's existing animals."

He smiles down at Luma. The morning sun highlights the golden patches in her white coat, living up to her name.

"Well, you know what this means, don't you?" I ask with mock seriousness.

"What's that?"

"Joe's going to be furious that he's no longer the only dog in my life."

Jack laughs, the sound echoing off the pastel buildings around the square. And— as much as I'm excited that the dogs will come to live at the castle— I'm also a little nervous. Adding a single animal to a home can create tension. An entire pack of dogs? That's something else. And I'm still not sure where I fit in the Duke's life yet. He's made it clear he's "courting" me, but I don't actually know how he feels about me. Is this just a casual fling? Or will we grow into something more?

Adding a dog might be just the kind of life stressor that makes— or *breaks*— us.

CHAPTER
Two

"THE TOURISM BOARD is thrilled you're joining us today," Maggie says, her blonde braids bouncing as she walks. She's wearing a tailored blue blazer over a crisp white blouse, looking every bit the efficient Head of Household she is. "They're a motley crew, and lately, they've been more mutiny than meeting. Honestly, I could use backup."

"Oooh, is that why I'm here?" I ask, keeping an eye on Joe as he ambles beside me. "I thought you just needed someone to take notes."

Maggie laughs. "It doesn't hurt that you're dating the Duke. I'm hoping that bringing a local celebrity to the meeting will distract them long enough I can get some work done."

"Well, I hope they're not expecting royal expertise," I say, tugging lightly on Joe's leash as he veers toward a nearby café to investigate the scent of freshly baked bread. Beside him, Luma walks in a perfectly straight line, already better on a leash than Joe. "Joe and I are still learning the difference between a duchy and a principality."

"You're both coming along splendidly. Practically Royal

experts by now! And Luma's doing so well," Maggie beams, glancing down at the perfectly behaved Collie.

"I know," I smile. "I convinced Jack to part with her for an hour so I could take her out for a training walk." I click a noise-maker in my hand, then throw Luma a treat when she stops by my side. "If Jack had his way she'd remained untrained and feral, surviving on treats and pluck alone."

"It's a good thing she has you," Maggie nods seriously.

She pauses in front of a cheerful yellow building with a wooden sign reading "*Atwood Village Hall*" hanging above its arched doorway. The dogs enter first, then Maggie and me. Inside, a conference room has been prepared with a long wooden table surrounded by mismatched chairs. Sunlight streams through tall windows, illuminating dust motes dancing in the air. Five people are already seated, engaged in various conversations. All eyes turn to us—or more accurately, to Joe and Luma, who always get the attention in a room.

"Everyone, I'd like you to meet Rebecca Orange from Castle Atwood," Maggie announces with a warm smile. "She's our animal expert and will be joining our meetings as the castle's representative. She's brought two of the castle dogs with her today— Joe, and Luma."

Joe wags his tail politely, causing a ripple of reactions around the table. Luma arranges herself in a perfect "sit" position, waiting at attention. A thin man with wire-rimmed glasses visibly recoils, while a woman with blue and purple hair leans forward with interest. I recognize her as Pepper, the young anarchist I met just a couple months ago. I'm surprised to see her here— organized council meetings didn't seem up her alley.

Maggie gestures around the table. "Rebecca, meet the board."

She points to a woman with neatly pinned hair and an

overachiever's smile. "This is Matilda, our tourism board secretary."

Matilda perks up, clutching a notepad like it's a sacred text. "It's an *absolute* pleasure to meet someone from the castle," she says brightly. "I've been following the museum project closely. The Duke's vision is so... *inspiring*."

There's a breathlessness in her tone that makes my radar ping. *Relax, Rebecca,* I think to myself. *This is the downside of dating a Duke. All the women have crushes on him. Every rose has its thorn.*

"And this is Andre," Maggie says, nodding toward a rail-thin man wedged against his chair like he's avoiding contagion. "He owns the bookshop on High Street."

"Dogs have no place in official meetings," Andre says flatly, eyeing Joe like he's a biohazard. "Their teeth make them a hazard. You might as well invite a dinosaur to high tea."

"Couldn't," I say, straight-faced. "My T-Rex likes to sleep in. Couldn't wake him up before noon."

He doesn't laugh.

"Joe is a trained service animal," I add, my tone cooling. "Luma's still in training, but she's top of her class."

I neglect to mention that it's a class of one. Andre sniffs and looks away, unconvinced.

Maggie quickly moves on. "You remember Pepper."

Of course I do. No one forgets Pepper. She's draped in black, fishnet sleeves on her arms, and a defiant glint in her eye. Beside her is a guy with safety pins in his jacket and boredom carved into his posture.

"Lawrence," she says, jerking her head toward him. "My boyfriend. He's documenting the slow collapse of civilization."

Lawrence doesn't look up from his phone.

"We're here to hold the board accountable," Pepper

announces, scanning the room like she's ready for battle. "If this village is going to sell its soul to tourism, we want to make sure the profits go to the people, not just the castle."

Maggie offers a diplomatic smile. "The Duke requested a range of perspectives."

I nod, filing it all away. Matilda, the royal fanatic. Andre, the dog-hating grump. Pepper, the rebel with a clipboard. And Lawrence, the silent shadow.

Andre cuts in, eyeing the dogs with thinly veiled disgust. "I'd like to propose a new motion immediately: no pets allowed in tourist areas. They're unhygienic and destructive."

Joe looks up at Andre with liquid brown eyes that could melt the coldest heart, then sighs deeply and rests his massive head on my foot.

"I second the motion," Matilda says quickly, though her eyes never leave my face. "Not because of Joe, of course— he seems lovely— but for the overall tourist experience."

"All motions need to be on the agenda first," Maggie reminds them gently, opening her folder. "Let's start with item one: updates on increased tourism activity."

Under Maggie's careful direction, the meeting begins. Matilda takes furious notes but glances at me every few minutes with curiosity. Andre keeps as much distance from Joe as the confined space allows. Pepper interjects with critical questions about exploitation and authentic experiences, while Lawrence occasionally shows her something on his phone, prompting her to roll her eyes.

"The new Royal Museum has been our biggest draw," Matilda says, brightening as the conversation turns to castle-related tourism. "People are fascinated by the monarchy's history. Perhaps we could increase castle tours? Or add special events featuring the Duke himself? I think the people would love to see a *real* royal engaging in the community."

There's that tone again—a breathless quality when she mentions Jack that makes me sit up straighter.

"The Duke maintains a busy schedule," Maggie replies smoothly. "But he's committed to supporting village initiatives from behind the scenes."

"He's so dedicated to public service," Matilda sighs, clasping her hands together. "Did you know he studied sociology at university? His thesis on community-based governance models was revolutionary. I've read it three times." There's a glint in her eye that makes me wonder if she's read more than just his thesis.

Lawrence snorts and mutters something to Pepper, who elbows him sharply.

Maggie catches my eye with a small, knowing look before redirecting the conversation. "Perhaps we should move on to the new business item— the proposed 'Day of Love' event?"

"Yes!" Matilda exclaims, suddenly animated. She pulls out a folder stuffed with papers and spreads them across the table. "Valentine's Day is approaching, and I thought we could transform the village into a romantic destination. Heart-shaped decorations throughout the square, special menus at restaurants, flower stalls, perhaps even a dance in the evening."

"How original. Commercializing love to sell overpriced meals and tacky souvenirs," Pepper mutters, but I notice she's paying attention despite her cynicism.

"It could be tasteful," Andre offers. "Atwood has authentic historical connections to romantic literature. Lord Byron supposedly visited in the 1800s."

"The castle could host a special exhibit on royal romances throughout history," Matilda suggests, her eyes shining. "Perhaps the Duke could give a talk on historical courtship customs? Or host a special tea?"

"The Duke isn't particularly interested in being the center of attention," I find myself saying. "He prefers supporting community initiatives that highlight local businesses and artisans."

Matilda turns to me with unexpected intensity. "You seem very familiar with the Duke's preferences."

The room falls silent. Even Lawrence looks up from his phone.

Maggie clears her throat. "Rebecca and the Duke have been working closely on the animal conservation programs at the castle."

"Very closely," I add, feeling an unexpected protective instinct.

Matilda leans in, curious. "So the magazine covers *are* true? You're dating the Duke?"

"Yes," I say, shrugging.

The reaction around the table is immediate. Andre's eyebrows shoot up. Pepper smirks knowingly. Lawrence finally puts his phone down. But Matilda's face undergoes the most dramatic transformation— shock, disbelief, then something that looks alarmingly like calculation.

"I thought maybe that was a lie," she says, her voice higher than before. "The magazines make things up sometimes."

The way she emphasizes the word "lie" comes with a sting. It's as if she doesn't think I'm good enough to be dating the Duke. *Rebecca, bite your tongue,* I remind myself, trying not to say something I'll regret later. I clear my throat and shrug my shoulders before saying, "Look, I know my hair was bad in those photos, but now that you've met me in person, I'm sure you'll agree I'm quite the catch."

Andre laughs and Pepper gives me a thumbs up, but Matilda just offers a cold smile. The smile doesn't reach her eyes, which stay glassy and cool. She shuffles her papers.

"The Day of Love sounds like a wonderful initiative," Maggie says brightly, rescuing me from the awkward moment. "What activities were you considering, Matilda?"

Matilda snaps back to attention, though her movements seem jerky now. "Yes, well, I've prepared a complete proposal." She distributes copies to the room, passing mine across the table last. "I'm thinking heart-shaped lights strung across the square, a lovers' photo booth, perhaps a village-wide treasure hunt with romantic clues..."

As she outlines her elaborate plans, I notice her enthusiasm seems almost feverish now. *She's really into this idea*, I think.

"The grand finale could be a romantic ball," she continues, "perhaps at the castle? With the Duke in attendance, of course. Historical royal romances as the theme—"

"I think we should keep the focus on the village businesses," Maggie interjects gently. "That's where the economic benefit is most needed."

"Of course, but having the Duke—and his girlfriend—" Matilda glances at me with a tight smile, "—would draw considerably more attention and visitors."

Joe shifts at my feet, sensing my discomfort. I reach down to scratch behind his ears, grounding myself in his solid presence.

"I think what Maggie means," I say carefully, "is that the event should celebrate the village itself, not turn into a royal spectacle. Maybe you could hold the event in the village square instead of at the castle? Jack—the Duke—is very mindful about not overshadowing local initiatives by making them centered on the Royals instead of the people."

"How considerate of him," Matilda says with a brittle brightness. "You must tell me sometime how you two met. It sounds like such a fairy tale."

Before I can respond, Pepper interjects. "If we're doing this capitalist love-fest, can we at least ensure some proceeds go to community services? Maybe a donation program for the homeless shelter in the next village over?"

I shoot her a grateful look for the subject change.

The meeting continues with discussions of budgets and

logistics. As we wrap up, action items are assigned and a follow-up meeting is scheduled. The meeting is so boring I'm about to fall asleep, but then— something terrible happens.

Andre stands, stretching his arms, and— somehow— as he's bending over, something fuzzy drops onto the ground. I bend over to look at it. It almost looks like a hamster, or a pet. Then, I notice Andre frantically patting his head— which is suddenly... *bald.*

It hits me. *Andre's toupee has fallen on the floor.* It's a good toupee. I didn't realize when we entered he was even wearing one. No one else seems to have noticed yet, and Andre's about to reach for the hairpiece when a familiar bark echoes through the room.

I look down, only to realize that Luma has disappeared. Joe is still sitting patiently by my feet, but Luma's taken off. I look back toward Andre, and spot the dog at once. She's running across the room— with Andre's toupee in her *mouth.* He chases her like a pig on a farm, trying to catch her, but Luma is too quick. She slips from his grasp, leaping in the air. She clearly thinks this is a game and that Andre's enjoying it.

"Come— here— you awful— mutt!" Andre shouts, trying to cover his bald head while also reaching for the toupee.

Across the room, laughter echoes. Matilda gasps, but can't stop chuckling. Pepper and Lawrence point at the dog, taking out their cell phones to video the event. Maggie looks at me, horrified, and I echo the sentiment.

This is bad. Really bad.

"Stop chasing her!" I shout, trying to help. "That will only make her run more. Luma— cookie!" I throw out a treat and Luma immediately drops the toupee, running toward me to get a snack.

Andre grabs the toupee from the floor and slams it on his head. It sits akimbo, looking all wrong after being chewed on by Luma. Andre has his hair back, but the damage is done. He marches toward me and thrusts a finger in my face.

"That dog is a menace," he hisses, his toupee now listing to the left like a sinking ship. "And I'll see to it she's banned from the village... permanently."

With that, he marches off. Luma looks up at me with big, angel eyes, completely unaware of what she's done.

CHAPTER
Three

"WELL, THAT WAS EMBARRASSING," I say later as Maggie and I make our way down the cobblestoned streets of the village. "Luma's training might take a little bit more effort than I had planned." I take a bite of the croissant in my hand.

"I thought she was perfect," Maggie beams, reaching down to pet the top of Luma's head. Luma trots along beside Joe, both of their tongues hanging out as we bounce down the road. Maggie sips the iced rose-latte she just picked up at *Cafe de Flore.* "If I didn't know any better, I'd think you trained her to purposefully rip the toupee off stupid Andre's head. He's been such a pain during these tourism board meetings. At least today I got to laugh!"

"He was really mad," I shudder, remembering the way Andre stormed out of the building in a huff. "I hope he doesn't try to get us exiled from the village."

Maggie stops in front of a cute, brown building, taking in the familiar pastel shutters. A stained glass window beams back at us. "I guess Andre won't be one of our customers..." She smiles at me.

On top of the door, a shiny new sign reads:

"Royal Investigators"

The royal crest is positioned above the words, indicating our official status. This office is something Maggie and I have been working on for awhile— it's our pride and joy.

"It's just like Jack to let us share our work as investigators with the village," I sigh, the thought of Jack sending a peaceful ripple up my back. "Now, we can solve mysteries for everyone, not just the castle."

"I *still* think our services shouldn't be free of charge—" Maggie grumbles.

"Maggie," I roll my eyes. "It's a service to the community!"

"I know, I know," Maggie sighs. "And it *was* kind of Jack to fund the opening of our office. Just don't tell him the only reason I wanted an office space in the village was to be closer to drinks and snacks at *Cafe de Flore.*"

"Your secret stays with me," I agree.

We step into the office, getting ready for an honest day's work. The space is cozy— nothing like the cavernous halls of Castle Atwood— but it feels right, somehow. A perfect blend of royal polish and village charm, just like the partnership Maggie and I have formed over these past few months. The building used to be an old bookshop in the heart of Atwood Village. The exposed wooden beams crossing the ceiling give it character, while the stone walls keep the space cool even as summer approaches. Maggie has somehow managed to blend castle elegance with village practicality— mahogany desks that would look at home in a royal study sit atop colorful handwoven rugs from the village market. The walls feature a mix of formal portraits of Monrovian royalty alongside framed newspaper clippings of local events.

"Joe, Luma— nap time!" I point to a dog bed in the corner,

and Joe and Luma run toward it. They arrange themselves like pretzels around each other, curling into the spot for a peaceful midday siesta.

My desk faces the window overlooking the cobblestone street, while Maggie's sits opposite, giving her a view of anyone coming through our door. Between us stands a small round table with four chairs—our "consultation area," as Maggie grandly calls it.

Because most of our time is spent at the castle and we're only at the office in-person a couple days a week, we've put a slit in the door attached to a mailbox for villagers to leave requests for assistance from the Royal Investigators.

"Anything?" Maggie asks, watching as I open the mailbox.

"Nothing today," I say, shrugging. "Apparently the town of Atwood is on its best behavior."

Just then— as if the Universe heard me— the bell above our door jingles, and Zacharia bursts in, his lanky frame practically vibrating with enthusiasm. He's clutching a newspaper and wearing the biggest grin I've seen on him since he managed to capture a photo of me with the Duke outside *Le Petit Scone* after the building was set on fire.

"Miss Orange! Ms. Lefevere!" He bounds toward us like an eager puppy. "I had to come thank you personally!"

Maggie rises, professional as always. "Zacharia, good morning. Would you like some tea?"

"No, no, I can't stay long. I need to get back to the newsstand." He holds up a gossip magazine. "But I wanted you to see this first."

I take the paper, scanning the headline: "Royal Investigators Crack Village Vandalism Case."

Beneath it is a surprisingly flattering photo of Maggie and me standing in front of Zacharia's newsstand, looking appropriately detective-like. I have to admit, we make a good team

—Maggie's polished professionalism balancing my more direct approach.

"Page three has the whole story," Zacharia says proudly. "I wrote it myself."

I flip to page three, where the headline "*Castle Expertise Extends to Village Crime-Solving*" spans the top of the page. The article details how we tracked down the teenagers responsible for vandalizing Rodrigo's newsstand last week. It wasn't exactly a challenging case—the culprits had left behind a distinctive shoe print that matched the limited-edition sneakers worn by the suspect and his friends—but it was our first official village case.

"*Castle investigators lend their talents to the villagers for free, as an extension of the Duke's modern government policy,*" Maggie says, reading over my shoulder. "This is great, Zacharia! I feel famous."

Zacharia beams. "I wanted to do you justice after you helped me so quickly. It would have taken Officer Basilier weeks to get around to investigating, if ever."

"Well, we're happy to help," I say, handing the paper back to him. "That's why we're here— to extend the castle's resources to the village."

"And I promise," Zacharia says, lowering his voice conspiratorially, "when I write about you and the Duke from now on, I'll be very fair. Only the nicest photos. No more unflattering angles. I've figured out you look better from the left side than the right."

I nearly choke on my coffee. "Thank you, Zacharia," I say, mustering as much enthusiasm as I can. "I'm horrified, but thank you. From this moment on, I will only talk to people if they're standing on my left side."

Zacharia winks. "Oh, don't take it the wrong way. Everybody has a good side and a bad side."

Before I can formulate a response that doesn't sound like teenage denial, the door flies open again. This time, there's no cheerful bell jingle— just the sharp crack of wood hitting stone as the door slams against the wall. The sound makes Joe and Luma leap up from the dog bed they're sharing, both of them at the ready.

Officer Basilier stands in the doorway, her petite frame somehow filling the entire entrance. Her police uniform is impeccably pressed, badge gleaming, and her expression suggests she's just bitten into something extremely sour.

"Miss Orange. Ms. Lefevere." Her clipped greeting lands like small stones.

Maggie rises smoothly. "Officer Basilier, what a pleasant surprise. Would you—"

"I'm not here for pleasantries," Basilier cuts her off, striding into the office. She surveys our space with narrowed eyes, as if searching for contraband. "I'm here on official business."

"Uhm," Zacharia says, sensing the discomfort in the room. "I just remembered I have something really important to get to at the newsstand. Rebecca, Maggie…" He pauses, eyes wide with fear, then whispers, "Good luck!" He rushes out the door and onto the street, making me jealous that he gets to escape Officer Basilier.

"What can we help you with, Officer?" I ask. Something fuzzy presses up against my leg, and I look down to find Joe. Beside him is Luma, mirroring his seated position. They've moved from the dog bed across the room and are sitting at my side, both of them alert.

"You can help by explaining why you're running a detective agency in a residential zone," she says, flipping open her notebook.

"Excuse me?" Maggie's professional composure slips slightly.

"This building," Basilier continues, tapping her pen against her notebook, "is zoned residential with allowance for literary retail only. Your... Royal Investigators service... does not fall under that classification."

"We have all the necessary royal permits," Maggie says, moving toward her desk. "The Duke himself authorized—"

"Royal permits don't supersede village ordinances," Basilier interrupts. "Castle authority ends at the village boundary. Here, you follow village rules."

I can see Maggie's diplomatic smile straining. "There must be some misunderstanding. We completed all the paperwork the village clerk provided."

"The clerk isn't the zoning board." Basilier produces an official-looking form from her pocket and slaps it onto the round table between our desks. "This is a notice of violation. You have forty-eight hours to cease operations or apply for a proper zoning variance."

I step forward to examine the form. "And if we don't?"

Basilier's thin smile doesn't reach her eyes. "Daily tickets. Two hundred euros each. Plus potential closure by court order."

Maggie joins me at the table, scanning the document. "This can't be right. We specifically asked about permits when we leased the space."

"Then you asked the wrong questions." Basilier adjusts her hat, looking almost pleased. "The Royal Family may think they can extend their reach into the village whenever they please, but some of us still respect proper procedure." She steps forward, her face flushing. "This village doesn't *need* a Royal Investigator service. The Police are doing a perfectly fine job."

The undercurrent of disdain in her voice isn't subtle. But I've come to expect nothing other than hostility from Officer Basilier. She doesn't like the Royals, and she *certainly* doesn't like me. Still, I try to stay on her good side.

"We'll look into this immediately," I say, keeping my tone neutral. "Thank you for bringing it to our attention."

Basilier looks almost disappointed that I didn't argue. "See that you do. I'll be back in exactly forty-eight hours." She turns to leave but pauses at the door. "And Miss Orange? Perhaps remind your... employer... that his title doesn't exempt him from following local regulations. Even if his *girl-friend* fancies herself a detective."

The door closes behind her with a definitive click.

"Well," Maggie says after a moment of stunned silence. "That was unpleasant."

I pick up the violation notice. "She's not just enforcing regulations. This is personal."

"But the papers are legitimate, unfortunately. There's a proper court seal and everything."

I move to the window, watching Officer Basilier striding down the cobblestone street, stopping to issue what appears to be a parking ticket to an unfortunate delivery truck. "So what do we do? Apply for this variance?"

Maggie is already tapping on her tablet. "I'm looking at the zoning regulations now. A variance application requires approval from the village commerce council, which only meets monthly." She frowns. "The next meeting is three weeks away."

"And in the meantime?"

"Daily tickets, apparently," she says grimly. "Unless..." Her fingers fly across the screen. "There might be a workaround. If we register as a cultural outreach program of the castle rather than an independent business, we might qualify for an exemption."

I turn back from the window. "Is that actually a thing?"

"Not exactly," Maggie admits. "But I can draft the paper-work to make it look official enough to buy us time. The Duke can sign off on it this evening when you have dinner." She gives me a knowing smile.

I roll my eyes but can't help returning her smile. "So we create this cultural outreach documentation, then what?"

"Then I pay a visit to the village clerk. Luckily, I know the clerk's weak spot. Let's just say it's flaky, buttery, and comes in a pink box from Chef Renauld."

"Tell Chef Renauld we're going to need her best baking," I say, glancing out the window. I can just make out Officer Basilier disappearing around the corner. "It's going to take more than croissants to fix this mess."

CHAPTER

Four

THE FIRE CRACKLES in the castle library, throwing golden light across ancient books and my sock-covered toes, which currently rest in Jack's lap. Luma lies curled like a furry crescent moon on the rug in front of the hearth, her fluffy tail twitching in sleep. Joe, my Tibetan Mastiff, snores beside her like a furry freight train. It's a peaceful evening, in that sacred, post-dinner lull where time doesn't matter and books are the only obligation.

Jack flips a page in his history book, still massaging my ankle without thinking. "Did you get to the part where the murderer escapes through the priest hole?"

"Not yet," I say, keeping my voice low, not to disturb the dogs— or the vibe. "I'm still at the part where everyone's lying and no one's alibi holds water. You know, the good part."

He grins, eyes still on the page. "The part where you'd solve it in five minutes and ruin the ending for everyone else."

"Guilty." I sip my wine and sigh. "And you'd write a treatise on the class structures that created the murderer in the first place."

Jack chuckles, his salt-and-pepper hair catching the fire-light like something out of a portrait. "We make a good team, Orange."

"That we do, Your Highness."

We fall into silence again, save for the sound of rain tapping the tall windows and Luma's soft, sleepy huffing. It still surprises me how easily we've fallen into this rhythm—shared meals, half-read books, quiet companionship. The so-called Party Prince has become my favorite introvert.

Jack reaches for the wine. "More?"

"Always."

He pours, and we return to our pages. A perfect night. Until his phone buzzes on the table between us.

He glances at the screen, and something in his expression shifts. He reaches for it, already standing. "It's Maggie."

Maggie never calls at night. Ever.

I pull my feet from his lap. Luma's ears perk up immediately, and she rises, padding over to Jack with soft clicks of claw on stone.

"Hello?" he says, turning toward the window.

His body stiffens like someone's struck him. One hand grips the window frame, steadying himself. The firelight hits his face just as it drains of color.

"I— yes," he says quietly. "When?"

Luma noses his hand, whining softly. He pets her head softly, cradling her long nose in his hand as if he wants to help her hold her own head up.

"I see. Of course. Please tell the Queen I'll leave tonight. Thank you, Maggie."

He ends the call slowly, as if reluctant to hear the silence that follows. Then he turns back toward me— and I know before he says a word.

Jack's voice is low. "My uncle— The King— is dead."

I stand, heart dropping. "Oh, Jack…"

"Heart attack. During a meeting with an advisor. Maggie

said it was immediate." He sits down heavily, Luma pressing herself against his leg. His hand finds her head and grips the thick fur. "I saw him last week. He was laughing. *Laughing*."

I cross the room and kneel beside him. "I'm so sorry."

"He was sixty-two," Jack says numbly. "He always seemed… indestructible. My Aunt is the blood heir to the throne and in charge of running the country, so Monrovia will be alright. But my family…"

Luma noses his face, sensing the shift in energy. Jack finally blinks and scratches behind her ear, letting her anchor him.

"He was the reason I studied sociology," he murmurs. "Told me if I wanted to modernize tradition, I needed to understand it first. Brilliant man. Stubborn as a goat."

"He supported you," I say gently.

Jack nods once. "Even when he hated my ideas. He still backed me."

We sit in silence, Luma now sprawled across both our feet. Joe lifts his head too, watching Jack with big, concerned eyes. Outside, the rain deepens, as though the sky has gotten the news too.

"I need to leave tonight," Jack says suddenly. "My aunt— The Queen— will need support. And funerals… they're complicated when crowns are involved."

I stand. "I'll ask Enrique to bring the car around. Maggie will meet you?"

"She's already mobilizing everything." He pauses, then looks at me, guilt creeping across his face. "Oh no. Luma— I have to leave her and I've only just gotten her." He bends down, taking the dog's face in his hands. "She'll think I've abandoned her. And we've only just met."

The dog isn't the only one who will miss you, I think, trying not to roll my eyes. Jack and I haven't been dating long enough for me to feel secure in our connection. What if he goes back to visit his family and runs into an old flame there?

Stupid Rebecca, I shake my head. *The man is grieving and you're worrying about nothing.*

"I'll look after Luma," I say immediately. "Personally. She'll stay with Joe and me in my apartment."

"I can't possibly ask—"

"You're not, I'm offering! They're best friends anyway." I nod at the pair of dogs, who are seated side by side, concerned looks on their faces.

Jack exhales, a shaky, grateful breath. "Thank you. I know she's a handful."

"She's a sweetheart. Joe's been a terrible influence anyway."

Jack almost smiles. "He has, hasn't he?"

"By the time you get back he'll have taught her a dozen tricks. Bad ones, of course. Like how to steal cookies off the counter."

He crosses to me and places both hands on my shoulders. "Thank you, Rebecca." He kisses me, and my brain stops working.

"I'll let you know how the ceremonies proceed." Jack nods, his expression darkened by grief, softened by something else. "I'll call as soon as I land."

He turns to leave, but Luma whines sharply. He crouches to wrap his arms around her massive body, pressing his forehead to hers.

"I'll be back soon," he whispers into her fur. "Be nice to Rebecca and Joe. And don't eat the groundskeeper. I'm quite fond of Douglas."

She licks his cheek, and he stands. I watch as he leaves the library, shoulders squared again— no longer just Jack, but the Duke of Atwood, stepping into his duty.

The door clicks shut behind him.

I linger in the firelight, the spell of our evening broken. The wine has gone cold, the books abandoned. Joe comes to my side and leans against my hip. Luma lies back down but doesn't sleep, eyes fixed on the door.

I glance at Jack's book— *Monrosha: The First Queen of the People*. The pages fan out as if waiting for him to return.

Tomorrow I'll work with the animals on training at the hillside menagerie. Luma will need time, patience, and consistency to adjust to Jack's absence. And the castle, too, will need steady hands.

Because everything has shifted.

The King is dead. The Duke is gone.

And I'm still here— watching over a hound who's already missing her person. I bend down and scratch Luma's ears. "Don't worry, Luma," I say. "I miss him too."

CHAPTER
Five

SUNLIGHT STREAMS THROUGH MY WINDOWS, stirring the animals beside me— but it's Luma's quiet sadness that gets me moving.

Joe, ever the early riser, lets out a contented huff and stretches across the bed, thumping his tail against the mattress so hard it nearly knocks my alarm clock off the nightstand. Luma, curled beside him, blinks slowly, her head tilting in that thoughtful way of hers.

"Hate to break it to you both, but you have to earn your keep today," I say, scratching Luma behind the ears. Joe's tail thumps even faster.

Twenty minutes later, and we're crossing the castle grounds. Joe trots beside me, vibrating with morning energy, while Luma follows at a slower pace, her usual light step dulled. She's been off since the Duke left.

"He'll be back soon," I tell her softly, wishing I believed it as much as I want her to.

We round the rose garden, and the menagerie comes into view. Alfredo the giraffe is already watching us from inside his enclosure, his long neck craning toward my backpack.

"Yes, yes, I know," I say as he whinnies dramatically. "Absolutely starving. Practically withered away."

I pull out a lunch sack full of cooked penne pasta. Alfredo eagerly scoops it up with his long tongue. Luma keeps her distance, eyes wide, clearly still awed by his towering presence.

"Dont worry," I tell Luma, smiling at her. "You'll get used to the giraffe eating pasta. Joe sure did."

In answer, Joe bends down and slurps up one of the rogue noodles Alfredo has dropped. Luma approaches and sniffs his muzzle, wondering if she can get in on the action.

After feeding Alfredo and checking on the birds of prey in the aviary, I gather Joe and Luma for the highlight of our morning.

"Ready for the best part?" I ask. Joe lets out a joyful bark.

We head to the refurbished barn at the eastern edge of the property. I unlock the doors and call out, "Good morning, everyone!"

A chorus of excited barks greets me, paws scrabbling against the floor. These are the rescue dogs the Duke adopted from the Atwood animal shelter. It was surprisingly easy to find them homes with the staff at Castle Atwood. Maggie sent a simple email to the entire staff and— much to my surprise — so many staff members wanted a dog that we had to create a waiting list. Every single dog we rescued has been adopted out, which means the staff quarters are a little bit more chaotic than they used to be. At night, the dogs sleep in staff apartments with individual owners who've volunteered to adopt them. During the day, the staff drop them off at doggy day care for enrichment activities. And today? The dogs are on duty.

Joe and Luma perk up, whining as they spot familiar faces. I swing the doors wide, and the pack pours out—a controlled chaos of tails and tongues.

There's Winston, the three-legged border collie; Mouse, a

black-and-white terrier with mismatched eyes; Duchess, the elderly golden retriever with a noble gait; and nine more, each with a tale— or rather, a *"tail"*— of their own.

"Alright, team, let's learn the drill," I say, leading them toward the grazing field.

The sheep barely glance up as we arrive. I position myself at the field's edge. The dogs instinctively fan out.

"Let's get herding! Winston, left flank. Pepper, right. Joe, take the rear."

Joe moves with a quiet authority, his bulk gliding into position. The pack forms a living fence, guiding the sheep in a steady ripple of motion. Everyone follows Joe's lead— it's hard not to. He has so much charisma, he's impossible to ignore.

Luma hesitates. She glances toward me, concerned. The look on her face says she's not sure where she belongs.

"Luma, center," I call. "You can do it. Come on… center!" A beat of uncertainty— then, she springs into action, weaving through the formation with elegance. For a few moments, she forgets to be sad. The sheep move like a single woolly organism. When one strays, Duchess steps in, redirecting it with slow but sure steps.

"Perfect!" I call. "Hold position."

The dogs freeze as I close the pen gate. Then: "All done. Great job!"

The pack erupts into joyful chaos. I make sure to give each one praise, with extra affection for Joe and a lingering touch for Luma.

"The Duke would be so proud," I whisper.

Her ears droop slightly. She leans into me.

We return the dogs to the barn, where a staff member will look after them until their owners return later in the day.

Back at my apartment, the morning's energy fades. Joe and Luma make a beeline for the oversized dog bed in the living room—a memory-foam bed in the shape of a palace that I bought from Benjamin's pet shop in the village. He'd thrown in a matching blanket for free, calling it "the most comfortable bed for a royal dog." Joe and Luma jump over each other into the foam palace, and collapse into a heap of fur. Joe curls protectively around Luma. She licks his ear. Soon, they're snoring.

I smile, check the time, and realize I'm due for a meeting with Maggie.

"Okay, you two," I tell the dogs. "Can you be good while I head into town for a while?"

Joe opens one eye as I bend down to scratch his ear, but otherwise, offers no promise to be good. Luma, however, gives me a deep, longing gaze, and licks my cheek. She whines a little, almost like she doesn't want me to leave.

"It's okay, sweet girl," I tell her. "I'll be back in no time."

After one more glance at the dogs, I open the sliding doors that open into the rose garden, locking them tightly behind me. Once I'm sure the animals are tucked in safely, I start the peaceful walk over the castle bridge toward Atwood.

The cobblestone streets are sun-drenched and warm as I walk into the village, making my way past the fountain in the central square. I make a quick turn when I pass the statue of Monrosha and Rodrigo's newsstand, stopping outside our "Royal Investigators" office. The bell over our office door jingles as I enter.

"Tell me your morning was better than mine," Maggie groans.

I nod toward the notice-covered corkboard. Flimsy pieces of paper completely cover the cork surface, marring it in various shades of pink, white, and yellow. "Those all ours?"

She sighs. "Officer Basilier delivered them personally. Parking violations, zoning issues, permits we apparently never filed. She says she's been 'overlooking' them for weeks."

"And only just remembered them now?" I ask.

"Rebecca!" Maggie gasps. "I'm ranting and you're the one going through it. How's the Duke? Is he okay? I hated being the one to make that call about the King last night."

"He's holding up. Better than you'd think. It's Luma I'm worried about. She barely touched her breakfast."

"You're missing him too," Maggie says, eyes twinkling.

"I'm a very independent woman," I lie.

"An independent woman who deserves macarons," she declares, dragging me out the door and toward Café de Flore. "The Duke's lucky to have you. And I *know* he's grateful you're looking after Luma."

After wrapping up the day's business with Maggie, I start my walk home, weaving through the village's cobblestone streets. I cross the bridge toward the castle, waving at security as I enter through the main gates. The rose garden is in full bloom, the scent of flowers hanging in the air.

I stop at the sliding doors that belong to my apartment, thinking how lucky I am to live in such a beautiful place. I pull out my keys to unlock the door, only— something's wrong.

The door is already unlocked.

I lean in, examining the locking mechanism. It's been smashed with something heavy— a hammer, maybe. Metal pieces litter the ground.

My first and only thought is for the pets. Joe. Luma. My heart pounds.

"Joe! Luma!" I shout.

There's a loud woof from inside, and I slide the door open, revealing Joe. He charges me at the door, trembling, deep, frightened barks echoing through the room.

"Joe? What is it, boy?"

He races back to the living room, turning to make sure I follow. My skin prickles. Joe never panics.

I scan the room. Everything looks untouched. But the

foam dog bed in the shape of a palace is empty. The horrible truth hits me:

Luma is gone.

"Luma?" I call, my voice rising. "Where are you, girl?"

Joe whines and paws at the dog bed. Together, we tear apart my entire home, checking everywhere: under the bed, behind the couch, inside the kitchen cabinets. No Luma. Sometimes animals hide when they're afraid. But Luma is nowhere to be found.

"Someone took her," I whisper. "But why?"

My pulse quickens. It's not like Joe to let someone enter his property. He's a guard dog, after all. But then again, I've trained the viciousness out of him. He's used to Monique and the cleaning service coming and going, as well as repairmen. If someone entered the apartment with treats, I have no doubt Joe would give them the benefit of the doubt. Which means they must have taken Luma peacefully. If there'd been any sign of struggle— Joe would have attacked.

Maybe Luma escaped, I think, suddenly hopeful. It's possible Luma ran away when a stranger entered. She could still be on the grounds, hiding and afraid.

Joe is pacing now, whining louder.

"We need to look outside," I say, grabbing his leash. I put Joe in his harness, and together, we step into the rose garden, hunting for Luma.

We comb the grounds, whistling and calling for Luma. "Douglas!" I wave at the groundskeeper, who's tending the roses. "Have you seen Luma?"

Douglas shakes his head and grunts. "Not since this morning, when you let her chase the sheep."

Joe and I don't stop to explain, but instead continue our search. We try the animal menagerie, the gardens, and the kitchen. We ask everyone we encounter if they've noticed a dog on the loose, but no one's seen her.

After a failed search, we return home. Back at my apartment, I fight panic. Jack trusted me with his dog. And I've lost her.

Joe rushes to the dog bed again, snuffling deeply. He paws at something— a folded corner of paper.

I pull it out. A flyer.

"Monrovia's Annual Day of Love Festival," I read aloud. Hearts and flowers cover the page. I didn't notice it before— and it definitely wasn't there this morning.

I flip it over. There's a handwritten message scrawled on the other side:

Or else.

Joe nudges the flyer urgently, letting out a deep whine. My stomach drops as I understand what Joe is trying to tell me.

Someone left this. Someone *wants* me to see it. Luma didn't wander off. She was taken. Deliberately. And— somehow— her disappearance is connected to the Day of Love Festival.

I stare at the date on the flyer. Whatever this is, it's a message. Whoever did this has issued a challenge. I need to find Luma before the big event.

Joe howls beside me. I wrap my arms around his thick neck. I can tell he feels guilty for letting Luma go. Joe is a pacifist, and probably didn't realize the intruder was a threat until it was too late.

"It's okay, Joe," I tell him. "You didn't know. It's not your fault," I pause, admitting the truth. "It's… *mine.*"

Joe whines, his wet nose pressing into my shoulder.

"We'll find her," I promise him, and myself. "We'll get her back."

CHAPTER
Six

AN HOUR LATER, and the search for Luma continues. The castle library has transformed from a quiet sanctuary into the eye of a storm. Staff members enter and exit, offering reports on the areas of the grounds they've already searched. Maggie stands at the center of it all, her tablet abandoned on the main desk as she directs people with the efficiency of a battlefield commander. Joe sits anxiously at my feet, his massive form unusually still, as if he knows that Luma's disappearance has thrown the entire castle into crisis mode.

"We've checked the North Wing twice," Monique, the castle's head of cleaning services, reports to Maggie in a breathless tone. "Nothing."

Maggie nods sharply, making a note on a blueprint of the grounds she's spread across the desk. "What about the old storage rooms near the kitchens?"

"Chef Renauld had her entire staff check them. Nothing yet," Monqiue responds before rushing off to her next assignment.

I watch Maggie work, guilt gnawing at me like a physical pain. Luma is missing. And it happened on my watch. As the castle's animal expert, this falls squarely under my responsibility.

Jack will never forgive me, I think to myself.

"This isn't your fault, Rebecca," Maggie says, somehow sensing my thoughts without looking up from her blueprint. "You couldn't have known someone would steal a dog from the castle grounds."

"Steal is a strong word," I reply, though we both know it's likely true. "I'm still hoping she escaped somehow."

Maggie gives me a look that's gentle but doesn't sugarcoat anything. "Douglas confirmed the fence near the east garden was cut. And the flyer you found was an ultimatum. This wasn't an accident."

Joe nudges my hand with his massive head, offering comfort in his own way. All 250 pounds of Tibetan Mastiff seems to sense my distress, pressing against my leg with a quiet whine.

"Douglas is still searching the grounds," Maggie continues. "Enrique is driving the perimeter road again. He's expanded to checking the back routes toward the village."

The library doors swing open with enough force to make everyone jump. Officer Basilier strides in, her petite frame somehow filling the doorway with authority. Despite her small stature, the Officer projects an intensity that makes even the castle staff step aside.

"So," she announces, scanning the room with sharp eyes, "another incident at the castle. How convenient."

Maggie catches my aghast expression and whispers at me under her breath, "I'm sorry, Rebecca, but we have to report any crime on the grounds."

"To *her*?" I complain.

Maggie straightens her shoulders and steps forward. "Officer Basilier, thank you for coming so quickly. We've prepared a report of everything we know so far about Luma's disappearance."

Officer Basilier takes the offered folder but doesn't open it. "First a dead body, now a missing dog. Castle Atwood is becoming quite the center of criminal activity these days."

The reference to the recent murder on castle property makes me wince. Finding a body wasn't exactly the welcome I'd expected when I moved to Monrovia. Then again, I solved *that* murder. And I know I can find Luma.

I straighten my spine. At fifty-three, I've faced down charging rhinos and aggressive predators. One small-town officer with an attitude problem doesn't intimidate me. "I was appointed as Royal Investigator by the Duke himself after helping solve the last case, Officer Basilier. I can handle the search for Luma on my own."

"Hmm," The sound manages to convey both disbelief and disdain. "My department will spearhead this investigation. You and Ms. Lefevere will stay completely out of it. The last time you two played Detective, you nearly got yourself and the Duke killed in a fire."

I bite my tongue, knowing that arguing will only make things worse. "We just want Luma back safely."

"I'm sure you do." Basilier flips open the folder. "Now, walk me through exactly what happened."

For the next twenty minutes, we go through every detail. Throughout my explanation, Basilier's expression remains skeptical, as if she suspects I'm somehow involved. When I finish, she snaps the folder closed.

"I'll be investigating everyone with access to the grounds, including staff." Her gaze fixes on me. "Especially recent hires."

The accusation stings, but before I can respond, my phone rings. The screen displays "Duke of Atwood," and relief washes over me, followed by fear. I tried to reach Jack the moment Luma disappeared, but he's only now calling me back.

What if he never forgives me?

"Excuse me, I need to take this," I tell Basilier, stepping away before she can object.

"Rebecca," the Duke's voice comes through, sounding tired but warm. "I just saw your missed calls. Is everything alright?"

I move toward the window for privacy, but can feel Basilier's eyes boring into my back. "Jack— I— I have some bad news." For the first time all day, I feel tears welling up in my eyes.

"What's wrong?" His tone is urgent. He sounds panicked. "Are you okay? What happened?"

Guilt floods me anew. The Duke— Jack— is dealing with a family tragedy, and now I have to add to his burden. "It's not me— it's Luma"

There's a pause. "What about Luma? Is she sick?"

"She's missing, Jack." The words feel like stones in my mouth. "Someone took her from my apartment this morning. We have the police here now, and everyone's searching, but..."

His sharp intake of breath cuts through me. "Missing? You mean stolen?"

"Yes. There's evidence someone cut through the fence. They left a flyer about the upcoming festival with the words 'or else' written on the back." The words pour out of my mouth too quickly. "It seems like a threat. I don't know what they want. I had Luma with me constantly and only left her alone for a minute. My apartment doors were locked, and it looks like someone forced their way out…"

The line goes quiet for so long I wonder if we've been disconnected. Finally, Jack speaks again, his voice steady despite the emotion I can hear beneath it.

"Someone broke into your apartment. Rebecca, you could have been home when it happened. You could have been hurt—"

"I'm fine, but Luma— Jack, it's my fault—"

"You couldn't have known someone would target her." His tone softens. "And if anyone can find her, it's you. Your understanding of animals is why I hired you in the first place."

I press my forehead against the cool glass of the window, watching staff members continue their search across the grounds below. "I promise I'll find her, Jack. I won't stop until I do."

"I have no doubt. You're a Royal Investigator, after all."

"Even though Officer Basilier just ordered me to stay out of it?"

Jack makes a sound that might almost be a chuckle. "Especially because of that. Basilier is good at her job, but she doesn't know Luma like you do. Use your title if you need to. I'll back you up."

"I'm so worried about her—" I say, my voice choking as I picture Luma alone and afraid. "If they hurt her—"

"They won't," Jack promises me, his voice firm. "I picked a scrappy survivor, remember? My girl Luma is going to make it," he calls the dog his girl as if he's known her forever. "If they were going to hurt Luma they'd have done it then and there. Did they leave anything behind? A random note, or—"

"Just the flyer for the upcoming Day of Love," I say, mind still spinning. "If they want ransom, we could pay it. But they didn't leave any demands."

"I need to get home. To help you," Jack says. "I just— things aren't going well here with planning the funeral. The Queen is beside herself. I have to walk in the procession—"

"Come back as soon as you can," I say. "By the time you arrive, I'll have Luma home."

"I know you will," Jack's voice is warm on the other line. "Just a moment!" He shouts over his shoulder, frustration echoing across the line. "Rebecca, they're calling me but—"

"I miss you too," I tell him.

"Is mind-reading a skill all animal trainers possess, or only the beautiful ones?"

After we hang up, I turn back to find Officer Basilier watching me with narrowed eyes.

"Calling in royal backup?" she asks.

"Just updating the Duke on his dog's status," I reply evenly. "He's understandably concerned."

"I'll be interviewing staff individually. In the meantime, don't let anyone leave the castle grounds."

After she strides away, Maggie joins me by the window. "So what did the Duke say?"

I give her a small smile. "He said to find his dog."

"Despite Basilier's warnings?"

"Especially despite them." I straighten my shoulders, determination replacing guilt. "Let's get to work."

Maggie's eyes light up with the familiar spark that appears whenever we're about to bend rules.

———

A few hours later, the scent of coffee and pastries drifts from the interior of our Royal Investigators office. I unlock the door, Joe padding heavily behind me. His nails click against the wooden floorboards as he makes his way to the plush dog bed Maggie installed in the corner. It's the only piece of furniture that looks brand new— everything else has the comfortable, slightly worn feel of items acquired from the village's various antique shops.

Maggie is already here, pinning a map of Castle Atwood and the surrounding Village of Atwood to our investigation board. She turns when she hears us enter, her usually neat braids slightly disheveled from the day's stress.

"I brought coffee," she says, gesturing to two steaming

cups on the desk. "And I may have stress-purchased every pastry Henri had left at Le Petit Scone."

Sure enough, a box of assorted baked goods sits open beside the coffees. I gratefully take a twisted braid cake— the bakery's specialty— and sink into the chair behind the desk.

"Any news from the staff out searching?" I ask, tearing off a piece of the sweet, raisin-studded bread and offering it to Joe, who accepts it with surprising delicacy for such a massive dog.

Maggie shakes her head. "Basilier is still interviewing staff. Douglas found pawprints in the mud just past the fence heading toward the village, but— Rebecca—" Maggie cringes. "There were human sneaker prints next to them."

"Someone was with her," I say, shaking with anger. "And Luma's such a good dog— she probably just followed—"

"Enrique is still driving around, checking side roads," Maggie adds. "If they're out there he'll find them."

I nod, feeling the weight of my promise to the Duke. "We need to work fast. The longer Luma's missing, the colder the trail gets."

Maggie grins. "I love it when you get all official-sounding." She turns back to the board. "So, where do we start?"

I join her at the board, studying the castle map she's pinned up. "We start with motive. Who would want to steal the Duke's dog, and why?"

"Ransom?" Maggie suggests. "Luma is well-known throughout Monrovia. Everyone knows how much the Duke loves her."

"Possible," I agree, taking a marker and writing a word on the board:

RANSOM.

"But we haven't received any demands yet."

"What about revenge? Or someone who's trying to hurt the Duke emotionally?"

I add another possible motive to the board:

REVENGE.

"That broadens our suspect pool considerably," I think out loud. "The Duke must have political opponents."

"He does," Maggie confirms, "but most are too concerned with their public image to do something as despicable as stealing a beloved pet." She pauses, tapping her pen against her lips. "What about the tourism board?"

The pieces click together in my mind as I understand what Maggie's getting at. "They're the ones in charge of the Day of Love," I think aloud. "That flyer that was left behind— have any been distributed to the public yet?"

"None!" Maggie answers, excited. "Rebecca, they just came up with the design. No one has access to it yet except me, and the tourism board. That means—"

"Someone on the board was involved." I grab a fresh sheet of paper and pin it to the board. "Let's start there."

For the next few minutes, we compile a list of everyone on the Monrovian Tourism Board who attended yesterday's meeting. Maggie accesses their photos on the tourism board website and prints them out.

"First, Matilda," I say as Maggie pins her photo to the board.

In the picture, Matilda's wearing glasses, dressed in a conservative skirt and blouse that are tailored to her slim shape. Despite her unassuming appearance, there's an intensity in her enormous eyes that's unmistakable.

"She just moved to Atwood late last year," Maggie explains. "She's very involved in the community. From what I've heard, she spent all her money making the move— she was so determined to live in this area."

"That could be a motive," I say. "Maybe she thought stealing Luma could yield some ransom money." Using a piece of string, I connect Matilda's photo to her possible motive, the word "Ransom" written on the board. "What about Andre?"

Maggie pins up a photo of Andre. He's distinguished-looking in an expensive suit. "Andre Bellisario, treasurer of the tourism board. Owns the bookstore down the street. Happens to be old money, very traditional, and notably opposed to the Duke's plans to open the castle to increased tourism."

"Why would he oppose that? Wouldn't tourism be good for the economy?"

"Not if you're a traditionalist who thinks royal spaces should remain private," Maggie explains. "Andre believes the monarchy loses its mystique when it becomes too accessible to ordinary people."

"He also hates dogs," I add, remembering what he said at the meeting after Luma grabbed his toupee. "He threatened Luma at that meeting! He said he'd make sure she was never allowed in the village again!" My heart races. I'm *sure* Andre did it. "Maggie, he's the one. We have to go over there right now."

"Rebecca," Maggie shakes her head. "We have to approach this logically. You always say we need to look at the evidence."

Maggie's words make sense to me, but still— Andre is my number one suspect.

"Fine," I say, using another piece of string to connect Andre's photo to the word "Revenge" as his possible motive. "Who else do we have?"

Next comes Pepper's photo— dressed in black and red, with fishnets on her arms and dark makeup that makes her pale skin seem almost ghostly.

"She's only on the tourism board as a 'youth representative,' but she uses every meeting to push for dissolving the monarchy entirely."

"I can't picture her stealing a dog."

"Uhm, Rebecca," Maggie says carefully. "She recently attacked you with a smoke bomb and lit *Le Petit Scone* on fire."

"Fair point," I agree, remembering Pepper's past antics. I take another string and connect Pepper's photo to her possible motive, the word "Revenge."

"There's also her boyfriend," Maggie adds, pinning up another photo. "Lawrence."

The image shows a young man, maybe nineteen or twenty, with a sullen expression and punk-rock clothing. He looks utterly uninterested in everything around him.

"Lawrence doesn't care about politics like Pepper does," Maggie explains. "He was expelled from university recently— something about cheating on exams— and now he's just trailing after Pepper to her meetings."

"No strong motive on his own," I observe, "but he might help Pepper if she asked. Or..." A new thought occurs to me. "What if he needs money? Student loans?"

"That's good," Maggie says as I connect a piece of string from Lawrence's photo to the word "Ransom." "Pepper's too ideological to ask for money, but Lawrence might not have the same scruples."

I step back, studying our collection of suspects. I tap my marker against my palm, thinking. "We should add Officer Basilier."

Maggie raises an eyebrow. "You think the police officer investigating the case is actually behind it?"

"I think she made it very clear she has issues with both the castle and us," I reply, writing Basilier's name on a fresh card. "She resents that the castle operates outside her jurisdiction. And she was furious after we solved the last case."

"Which she failed to solve," Maggie adds, understanding

dawning. "You think she might have taken Luma to make you look bad? To prove the castle needs proper police oversight?"

"It's a theory." I pin Basilier's name to the board. "We can't rule anyone out at this stage." I take a piece of string and connect Officer Basilier's name to the word "Revenge" on the board.

Maggie steps back, surveying our work. Five suspects, each with two potential motives. It's a start.

"So, what next?" she asks, taking another sip of her coffee.

I consider our options. "We need to interview each of them, find out where they were this morning when Luma disappeared."

"Basilier won't like that."

"We're not interfering with her investigation," I insist. "We're just having friendly conversations with members of the tourism board, following up on yesterday's meeting. Completely innocent."

Maggie laughs. "And how do we explain questioning Officer Basilier?"

"We'll save her for last," I decide. "Maybe we won't need to question her if one of the others pans out."

Joe rises from his bed and comes to stand beside me, looking up at the board as if he understands every word we've said. I scratch behind his ears, drawing comfort from his solid presence. Outside, the night coats the town square like a thick blanket, the moon shining overhead. Maggie rolls her shoulders and stands. "We should get some rest. Early start tomorrow?"

I nod, looking one last time at our suspect board. I turn my attention back out the window, staring into the deep, black night. "I hate to picture Luma out there all alone," I say.

Maggie puts a gentle hand on my shoulder. "Don't worry, Rebecca. We're going to find her."

I hope Maggie's right. Luma's counting on us. And so is the Duke. The thought of letting him down makes my stomach turn. *How will he ever trust me after this?* The bracelet he gave to me sits heavy on my wrist. It's a family heirloom he had engraved just for me— a vote of confidence in our love. I hope Jack doesn't blame me for what's happened, but I don't see how that's possible, when I already blame myself.

What if Luma isn't the only thing I've lost?

CHAPTER
Seven

THE NEXT MORNING, the Village of Atwood greets us with cobblestone streets and pastel-colored storefronts that look like they belong on a postcard. I sip my lavender latte from *Cafe de Flore*, the floral sweetness a perfect companion to the crisp morning air. Joe trots beside me, focused on the job ahead. We're on our way to question the tourism board, and Joe's focused demeanor makes me think he knows our efforts today will help us find Luma. On Joe's left flank, Maggie takes a sip of her rose-hip iced tea, considerably less focused than he is.

"What's the plan, boss? Do we play coy or let them know right off the bat we're looking for a lost member of our pack?" Maggie asks, watching a bird in a tree overhead flit from branch to branch.

"Let's be direct," I strategize. "We'll be open about the fact that Luma is missing. That way, I can read their reactions and try to get a feel for who already knows something's wrong."

"I like the strategy," Maggie nods. "Humans count as animals, so use those trainer skills you have."

We turn the corner, arriving at the exterior of the tourism office. A bell clangs as we open the door, entering the inviting space. Racks of brochures display Monrovia's scenic attractions. Matilda greets us, a big smile on her face.

"Maggie!" She pulls Maggie into a close hug, then pauses when she sees me. "Rebecca," she says with less warmth. Then, she pulls me into her arms as well. "I'm so glad you two showed up again. It's only Andre and me today. Pepper and Lawrence are absent, per usual. We got in a little disagreement with them about the sustainability of paper flyers so they're probably boycotting us and—"

Without warning, Joe jumps onto Matilda and begins scratching at her blouse. Matilda shrieks, taking a step back.

"Joe!" I shout, shocked at his behavior. He never does anything like this. "Down!"

Joe reluctantly agrees to my orders, but his actions have shaken me. Then, it hits me: Maybe he smells something on Matilda. Something important.

"He could have hurt my blouse!" Matilda exclaims, wiping the dog prints off her shirt. "Or worse, *me*. He practically swallowed me whole."

"Don't worry," I say, "he only eats people who steal royal dogs."

Matilda freezes for a half-second before bursting into nervous laughter. "Oh! You're joking! He's never eaten anyone… right? And," she pauses, considering. "What do you mean 'steals royal dogs ?'"

"We're actually not here for the meeting," Maggie admits, cutting to the chase. "You remember Luma, the Duke's dog? She was taken from the castle grounds at night."

Matilda gasps, covering her mouth in shock. "That's— my goodness— that's horrifying. Who would take a dog? Is she alright? I mean, at the scene was there any—"

"No blood," I say. "No signs of a struggle. We think whoever took her still has her. We found pawprints in the mud that indicate she left with them."

Matilda puts a hand to her chest, exhaling. "I hope you

find her," she says earnestly. "The Duke must be crushed. I can't imagine. Is he… holding up alright?"

"It's been difficult," I say.

Just then, Andre enters, his toupee placed firmly on his head. He scowls as soon as he spots Joe. "You again," he snarls, offering a curt nod. "What can we do for the castle today?"

"We're looking for information about Luma," I say, watching his face carefully. "The Duke's dog is missing."

Andre mutters something under his breath that I don't quite catch.

"What was that?" I ask.

"Nothing," Andre answers.

"I'd like to know what you said."

"All I said was good riddance!" Andre snaps, his face turning bright red. "Why are we wasting board time on the disappearance of a dog? We've got more important things to address—"

"But it *is* such a shame," Matilda interjects, shaking her head. "Do you need help putting up flyers?"

"We just came to ask the tourism board questions," Maggie says. "What about Pepper and Lawrence? You said they didn't come in today?"

Andre sniffs disapprovingly. "They miss half our meetings on average. Typical. The younger generation has no work ethic."

"That's fine," I say, anger flooding my veins. Being in the same room with Andre makes me even more certain he's the kidnapper. His disdain for animals makes me dislike him even more than Officer Basilier. "Because *you're* my main suspect."

Maggie looks at me, her mouth dropping open. *I told her we were going to be direct,* I think, shrugging my shoulders.

The change in Andre's demeanor is instant. His back stiffens, and his hand unconsciously moves to touch his hairpiece. "Excuse me?"

"You threatened Luma last time we were here, when she stole your toupee. And now she's missing. Seems like a pretty open and shut case to me."

Andre's face flushes red. "That— that mangy creature— you're lucky I didn't press charges for assault!"

Joe chooses this moment to move closer to Andre, his massive head level with the man's waist. He's not doing anything threatening— just looking up with his gentle brown eyes— but Andre takes a step back anyway.

"You said you were going to make sure she was kicked out of the village for good! And now she's missing!"

"It was a figure of speech!" Andre's voice rises an octave. "I was upset! That dog ruined an expensive hairpiece! The humiliation— in front of everyone!" Andre's hands are shaking now. "But that doesn't mean I would do anything to harm the Duke's pet. I'm a respected community leader. My family lineage—"

"No one said anything about harming," I note. "Interesting that your mind went there."

Andre opens and closes his mouth like a fish out of water. "This— this is outrageous! I'm being accused—"

"No one's accusing you of anything," Maggie interjects smoothly.

Actually, I'm accusing him of everything! I think, resisting the urge to say it out loud.

"We're just gathering information," Maggie continues. I'm lucky to have a partner who can hold her composure even when I can't. "Where were you the night Luma disappeared?"

"I was at home, alone, reading," Andre says stiffly. "I live by myself, so no, I don't have anyone who can verify that."

I make a mental note of this. Not having an alibi doesn't make him guilty, but it's certainly convenient.

"Come now," Matilda says, throwing her hands in the air

as if she's trying to block our questions. "Nobody on the tourism board would have hurt Luma."

"That's funny," I say, turning to her. "Because whoever took Luma left a flyer for the Day of Love Festival on her bed. And the only people who had access to that flyer were members of the board."

"I don't—" Matilda steps back, surprised. "That's true— but why—"

"What on Earth could the festival have to do with a mangy dog?" Andre huffs. Then, he pauses, concerned. "Maybe we should cancel it, if it's causing some kind of attack on the Royal Family?"

Matilda squirms, horrified at the idea. "We can't *cancel* it!" She looks like she wants to say something else, but stops herself. Her eyes scan the carpet, searching for a reason the Festival can't be canceled. "Hundreds of villagers are counting on the chance to connect— to celebrate. To believe in love again one last time. They *need* this Festival to happen!" Matilda's expression is manic, her eyes wide. She leans in, looking at me intently. "This Festival could be the start of new romances. Of love that changes *lives*. We can't cancel it. People are counting on this."

Someone's been watching one to many rom-coms, I think to myself, shaking my head. Still, this project is her baby. I can understand how disappointing it would be to see the work erased overnight.

"Is there anyone who's reached out to the board with concerns about the Day of Love?" Maggie asks. "Anyone who asked the board to cancel?"

"Oh no, everyone is thrilled!" Matilda insists with force. "It's been universally praised. To be honest, I think it's boosted the Duke's image. His expected attendance raised the event's profile. He will still be coming?" she asks nervously. "I heard he left town, given the death of the King. I hope he'll be back—"

"Right now the Duke is concerned with mourning his uncle and finding his dog," I say, annoyed that Matilda would raise such a concern at a time like this. "Those are his priorities."

"Of course!" Matilda smiles, but beneath, I can see her annoyance. "I suppose the event will just have to go on without him. If you don't mind, actually, we should get to the meeting—"

"The flyers," I add, not willing to let Matilda go so easily. "You're sure there's no one but the tourism board that had access to them?"

"We haven't printed them yet," Andre confirms. "They're in our shared drive. It's just me, Matilda, Maggie, Pepper, and Lawrence."

"As I was saying earlier," Matilda adds, "We ended up in a little spat with Pepper and Lawrence over the flyers. They argued a digital flyer would be more environmentally friendly. We planned on paper flyers for convenience. I imagine that's why they're not here today. They're quite angry with us."

I exchange a glance with Maggie. We're definitely going to need to track down Pepper and Lawrence, the two absent tourism board members.

"Well, thank you both for your time," I say, finishing my latte. "We should get—"

Before I can complete my sentence, Matilda lunges forward and wraps her arms around me in an enthusiastic hug. I stiffen, not expecting the sudden physical contact. Over her shoulder, I see Maggie's surprised expression.

"I'm just so glad the Duke has Royal Investigators like *you* helping him," Matilda gushes, finally releasing me. Then she turns and gives Maggie an equally fervent embrace. "And you, too, Maggie! You both make such a wonderful team!"

Joe lets out a small whine, backing away from Matilda's excessive enthusiasm. Smart dog.

"Right," I say, taking a step toward the door. "We'll be in touch if we have more questions."

"Any time!" Matilda calls as we exit. "Anything for the Duke!"

The bell jingles as the door closes behind us. Joe, Maggie, and I stand on the sidewalk for a moment in silence.

"Well," Maggie says finally. "That was..."

"Weird," I finish for her. "That was deeply weird."

I glance back at the tourism office window, where I can see Matilda watching us, still smiling broadly. She gives an energetic wave when she notices me looking.

"I think we need to find Pepper and Lawrence," I say quietly. "It's strange they were absent today." Andre is still my top suspect, but I realize Maggie is right— I can't focus on him to the extent of excluding other possibilities.

THE BELL over the door of L'animalerie Indiana Bones jingles as we enter, and I can't help but smile at the life-sized cardboard cutout of Harrison Ford wielding a bullwhip that greets us. Benjamin's obsession with American movies is on full display, from the "Temple of Treats" dog biscuit display to the "Raiders of the Lost Bark" poster featuring a German Shepherd in a fedora. Joe immediately perks up, recognizing both the shop and the man behind the counter who keeps premium bacon treats in his pocket specifically for my enormous dog.

"Rebecca! Maggie!" Benjamin calls out, his slight French accent warming his words. He rushes from behind the counter, green eyes bright with enthusiasm. "And *bonjour,* Joe, my favorite four-legged customer!" He's already fishing in his pocket for the promised treat.

Joe sits obediently but can't contain his excitement. His tail sweeps across the floor with enough force to clear a small shelf of cat toys, which I quickly stoop to retrieve.

"Sorry about that," I say, rearranging the felt mice. "His tail has a mind of its own."

Benjamin waves away my apology. "This is nothing. Last week, Mrs. Bellingham's Great Dane knocked over an entire display of fish food. I was finding colorful flakes for days." He crouches down to Joe's level, offering the bacon treat on his flat palm. "For you, monsieur."

Joe takes it with surprising delicacy, considering his size. Benjamin scratches behind his ears, and Joe leans into it with shameless pleasure.

"Benjamin, we came to ask for your help," Maggie says, pulling out her tablet. "The Duke's new dog, Luma, has gone missing."

Benjamin straightens up immediately, his expression shifting to concern. "Missing? When did this happen? Have you checked the castle grounds thoroughly? Sometimes dogs find a nice spot to nap and—"

"We did," I interrupt. "But all we found was evidence that this is more than a runaway dog. We think—" the words get caught in my throat. I clear away the sadness, trying again, "We think someone kidnapped her."

Benjamin gasps. "Who would do such a thing?"

"We're determined to find out," I say. "Have you heard about any other missing pets in the village? Maybe a repeat offender is at work..."

Benjamin shakes his head, running a hand through his brown hair. "No, nothing like that. I would have heard—most pet owners in Atwood come through here at least once a week." He leans against the counter, thinking. "There was a cat named Pierre that Madame Belcourt was feeding... he went missing for a few days, but it turned out he was actually living a double life with the seamstress two streets over."

Despite our concern, I can't help but smile. "That'll teach her to trust a man. Guess we know where the term 'tomcat' came from."

"Precisely," Benjamin says with a grin. "But no, no other

missing dogs or cats reported to me." He drums his fingers on the counter. "Wait, I may have something that could help."

He disappears into the back room, and I take the opportunity to survey the shop more thoroughly. Benjamin has expanded his inventory since my last visit. There's a new section dedicated to exotic pet supplies— specialized heat lamps, terrariums, and food supplements that remind me of my work with the castle menagerie. The movie theme extends to every corner: "Jurassic Bark" dog toys, "E.T. the Extra Terrier-strial" beds, and "Star Paws" themed collars. Benjamin returns with a small box, his eyes lighting up with excitement.

"These just came in last week. Dog GPS tiles— the latest technology." He opens the box to reveal small square devices, no bigger than a quarter. "You attach them to your dog's collar, and you can track them through an app on your phone. The battery lasts for months, and the range is impressive."

Maggie and I both step closer to examine the devices.

"They're waterproof, shockproof, and virtually indestructible," Benjamin continues, clearly in his element. "I've been recommending them to everyone with escape-artist pets. When you find Luma, you can put one on her so this never happens again. If someone takes her in the future, you'll know where they go."

I wish I'd had this a few days ago, I think, trying not to be mad at myself for not purchasing one earlier. I pick one up to inspect it. It's lightweight but solid. "How much are they?"

"For you? And the Duke?" Benjamin waves a hand. "Free. This is a royal animal emergency. I want to help." Benjamin passes me two boxes. "One for Luma— when you find her— and one for Joe." He looks down at my canine companion lovingly. "Whoever did this might try to strike again. I don't want my best buddy disappearing."

The thought of someone taking Joe makes my heart race.

Benjamin walks us through the setup process, helping me download the app and pair the first tile to my phone. Then he carefully attaches it to Joe's collar, nestling it between the existing tags. Joe tolerates this with the patience of a saint, though his eyes never leave Benjamin's pocket where the treats reside. "There," Benjamin says, stepping back to admire his handiwork. "Now, wherever Joe goes, you'll know exactly where he is." He pulls out his phone. "See? He's showing up right here on the map." Sure enough, a small paw print icon appears on the digital map of the shop. I move Joe to the other side of the room, and we watch as the icon follows his movement with only a slight delay.

"This is brilliant," Maggie says, clearly impressed. "I should suggest these for all the castle animals."

"I wish Luma had been wearing one," I sigh, pocketing the second GPS tile. "It would make this so much easier."

"You'll find her," Benjamin assures us, his hand on my shoulder. "And when you do, you'll have this ready to go."

"Thanks, Benjamin," I say, genuinely grateful.

As we prepare to leave, Benjamin has one more idea. "You should make some flyers. Offer a reward. I can put one in my window—lots of pet owners will see it."

"That's an excellent idea," Maggie says, already tapping on her tablet. "I can design something right now."

While Maggie works on the digital flyer, Benjamin tells me about the latest action movie he's managed to import from America. His enthusiasm is infectious, momentarily distracting me from our search mission. By the time Maggie holds up her tablet to show us the finished design, Benjamin has promised to lend me his rare collector's edition DVD set that includes deleted scenes and director commentary.

The flyer Maggie has created is perfect—a clear photo of Luma looking regal and alert, the word "MISSING" in bold letters across the top, and details about where and when she was last seen. At the bottom, in slightly smaller text: "REWARD OFFERED."

"We can get these printed at the copy shop down the street," Maggie says.

We say our goodbyes to Benjamin, who promises to keep his eyes and ears open for any news about Luma. Joe receives one final treat before we head out the door, the bell jingling behind us.

Twenty minutes later, after a brief stop across the town square, we step out of the local print shop armed with a stack of freshly printed flyers. Maggie leads us on a route through the Village of Atwood to distribute them in the busiest areas. The cobblestone streets are swimming with afternoon shoppers, and many stop to ask about the flyers as we post them on community bulletin boards, lampposts, and in shop windows.

"This is good," I tell Maggie as an elderly couple promises to keep watch for the collie. "The more eyes we have looking, the better our chances."

Maggie nods, handing a flyer to a curious teenager. "The village is like one big family when it comes to helping each other out."

We make a left past *Cafe de Flore*, stopping at an ornate iron lamppost that towers over the street to affix a flyer to its surface. When we're done, Maggie pops into *Cafe de Flore* to give Jocelyn a stack of flyers, and she waves at me from behind the counter. *"Bonne chance,* Rebecca!" Jocelyn calls, her warm smile making me feel at home. "If anyone can find the dog, it's you and Maggie."

Maggie re-emerges, and we head across the square to look for other friendly businesses. Joe trots alongside us, occasionally stopping to sniff at interesting spots. I watch him with a new awareness, knowing I can check my phone at any moment to confirm his exact location. It's reassuring in a way I hadn't expected.

As we approach the newsstand, I spot Zacharia arranging magazines on the display rack. When he sees us, his face lights up in greeting. "Miss Rebecca! Miss Maggie!" he calls out, waving enthusiastically. He abandons his task and hurries over to us. "And Joe, the castle's most magnificent beast!" He gives Joe a respectful pat, having learned through trial and error that Joe prefers gentle greetings to exuberant ones.

"How's business today?" I ask.

"Steady," he replies, glancing back at the newsstand with obvious pride. "The summer tourism edition is selling well. What are those?" Zacharia gazes at the flyers in our hands. His curiosity is immediate, as always. It's what makes him so well-suited to the news business.

"The Duke's dog has gone missing," I explain, handing him one of the flyers. "We're hoping to spread the word throughout the village."

Zacharia studies the flyer with intense focus, his expression growing serious. "Missing?" He looks genuinely distressed. "When did this happen?"

As we fill him in on the morning's events, Zacharia nods thoughtfully, occasionally asking clarifying questions that demonstrate his newsman's instinct for details. "This is big news," he says when we finish. "Rodrigo always said that village news should take priority over international affairs because it's what affects people directly." He taps the flyer with his index finger. "I can put this on the front page of tomorrow's village edition."

"Could you really?" Maggie asks, clearly pleased by the offer.

"Absolutely! With a headline like 'Duke's Beloved Dog Missing—Village Search Underway' and Luma's photo right in the center." His eyes are bright with journalistic enthusiasm. "Everyone who comes to the newsstand will see it."

"That would be incredibly helpful, Zacharia," I say,

touched by his eagerness to assist. "The more people who know to look for her, the better our chances of finding her quickly."

This almost makes me want to forgive Zacharia for the terrible photo of me he put on the front page last month, I think to myself.

"Consider it done," he assures us, carefully folding the flyer and tucking it into his shirt pocket. "Top story tomorrow. I'll make sure of it."

"Thank you," Maggie says sincerely. "The Duke will be grateful."

Zacharia straightens his shoulders, looking both proud and determined. "If there's something people need to know, it's our job to make sure they know it." He sounds exactly like his mentor, and I can't help but smile at his earnest dedication.

"Rodrigo taught you well," I observe. "He'd be proud,"

Zacharia agrees with unabashed admiration. "I should get back to work, but I'll make this my top priority. Tomorrow morning, first thing, Luma's face will be on every paper in the village."

We thank him again, and he returns to his post with renewed energy, already making notes on a small pad he keeps in his pocket.

"Well," Maggie says as we walk away, "between our interviews this morning, the flyers, and tomorrow's newspaper coverage, we've made good progress."

I nod, feeling a cautious optimism building. "The village is mobilizing. If Luma is anywhere nearby, someone will spot her. It can't be easy to hide a dog that big."

Joe walks between us, his GPS tile securely attached to his collar, a tangible reminder of both our concern and our preparation. I reach down to stroke his massive head, drawing comfort from his solid presence. "Let's head back to the castle," I suggest.

"Not so fast," Maggie says, pointing across the square.

"Guess we know why Pepper and Lawrence didn't make this morning's meeting." She points across the square at a familiar blaze of blue hair, its owner handcuffed to a lamppost and shouting wildly. "Got enough energy to interview another suspect?"

"For Luma?" I say. "Always."

CHAPTER
Nine

I WATCH Pepper tug against her handcuffs, the metal clinking against the ornate iron lamppost as she adjusts her protest sign. The sign reads:

Tourism = Human Commodification

The words are painted in wobbly red letters across cardboard that's clearly been recycled from her last cause.

"Human commodification?" Maggie mutters, reading the sign out loud. "What on earth is she on about *now?*"

"I don't know," I answer. "But you have to admire her passion."

Joe walks beside me, his massive frame casting a shadow across the cobblestones as Maggie checks her tablet one last time. "Alright, let's go talk to Pepper. She's my favorite anarchist," Maggie says before adding, "she's also the *only* anarchist I know."

We approach the town square, where Pepper has stationed herself next to the bubbling fountain. The contrast between the quaint architecture and Pepper's fierce protest stance would be comical if the situation weren't so serious.

Pepper sees us coming and straightens her spine, lifting her chin defiantly. Her blue and purple hair catches the morning light, making her look like some exotic bird of prey. Her boyfriend Lawrence stands a few feet away, leaning against a brick wall, scrolling through his phone with practiced boredom. His punk rock attire— ripped jeans, studded leather jacket, and combat boots— seems calculated rather than authentic, like he's trying too hard to match Pepper's genuine rebellion.

Joe trots ahead of us, his tail wagging as he approaches Pepper. Despite her anti-establishment facade, I've noticed she has a soft spot for animals. As expected, her face softens momentarily as Joe nudges her free hand with his nose.

"Traitor," I whisper to him, but there's no real criticism in my voice. Joe's uncanny ability to read people has saved me more trouble than I can count.

"Good morning, Pepper," Maggie says cheerfully, as if finding someone handcuffed to public property is a perfectly normal start to her day. "Interesting choice of protest location."

Pepper rolls her eyes. "It's the most visible spot in Atwood. I want people to know what's happening here. The tourism board is a capitalist front designed to commodify the free movement of humans across arbitrary geographical boundaries."

"Pepper," I say, unable to resist, "you *do* know you're on the tourism board, right?"

"I'm infiltrating from within," Pepper says without missing a beat. "You can't dismantle the system without understanding its mechanisms."

"So you were pretending to be a real participant this entire time, but really were planning to destroy them?"

"Not exactly," Pepper blanches. "I actually was having a lot of fun when I first came to the meetings." There's a wistful look in her eyes, but she quickly shakes it away. She seems almost disgusted by her own enjoyment of a structured activity. "But they showed me what they're really about when they insisted on using paper flyers that kill trees! Even after Lawrence and I presented them with statistics about paper manufacturing and how it damages the environment. Right, Lawrence?"

Lawrence— who's sitting on the edge of the fountain— doesn't look up from his phone, but gives her a thumbs up.

Pepper raises her voice as a couple of tourists walk by, clearly hoping to recruit an audience. "Travel should be driven by cultural exchange, not economic exploitation!"

The tourists quicken their pace, clutching their guidebooks tighter.

"So that's why you two missed this morning's meeting?" Maggie asks, consulting her tablet. "To protest the board whose very meeting you were supposed to attend?"

"We had more important things to do," Pepper replies, tugging at her handcuffs as if to emphasize her commitment. "Lawrence and I were volunteering at the food bank."

I glance at Lawrence, who finally pockets his phone and acknowledges our presence with a nod that manages to be both dismissive and reluctant.

"All morning?" Maggie presses.

A flicker of concern passes over Pepper's face.

"What is this, an interrogation?" Lawrence finally speaks, his voice carrying the practiced disaffection of someone who's never had anything real to worry about. "Since when do castle staff get to question citizens about their whereabouts?"

Joe's ears prick up at Lawrence's tone, and he moves slightly closer to me. I place a reassuring hand on his massive head.

"We're just having a conversation," I say mildly. "And speaking of conversations, we'd like to talk to you both about the Duke's dog, Luma. She's gone missing. We think she's been kidnapped."

Pepper's expression changes instantly, the performative outrage replaced by what looks like genuine concern. "Kidnapped?! That's a violation of personal rights," Pepper says. Whatever her feelings about monarchy as an institution, I've never known her to extend her animosity to animals. "Have you checked the village? Maybe she ran away."

"We're exploring all possibilities," I say, which is diplomatic phrasing for 'we have no idea where she is.' "Have either of you seen her in the past twenty-four hours?"

"No," Pepper says firmly, looking me directly in the eyes.

Lawrence shakes his head. "Haven't seen her."

Joe walks over to Lawrence, circling him slowly, nose to the ground. Lawrence shifts uncomfortably.

"Could you call your dog off?" he asks, a slight edge to his voice.

"He's just being friendly," I reply, though I know perfectly well that Joe is doing his own form of investigation. His behavior around Lawrence interests me— Joe typically makes immediate judgments about people, either befriending them enthusiastically or maintaining a polite distance. This circling, assessing behavior is unusual.

"So, the food bank," Maggie continues. "Which section were you working in exactly?"

"Why does it matter?" Lawrence challenges.

"Just making conversation," Maggie says with a smile that doesn't quite reach her eyes.

"We were sorting canned goods," Pepper says quickly. "Look, if this is about the tourism meeting, I've made my position clear." She jerks her handcuffed wrist for emphasis. "The board is killing trees for a glossy new brochure for the Day of Love. A stupid festival! And why are we even *having* this festival anyway? Because Matilda's obsessed with the romance of life? Please. We could be making a *real* difference, funding food banks and a community garden."

Maggie and I exchange a glass. *She mentioned the brochure*

again. It can't be a coincidence that the board's falling out had to do with the very flyer left on Luma's bed.

"Funny you keep mentioning the flyer," I say, shaking my head. "Considering the thief left a copy of the flyer for the festival on Luma's bed."

Pepper freezes for a fraction of a second before recovering. "You guys can't seriously think I'd take a dog?"

"Pepper," I say. "I seem to remember you threw a smoke bomb at me not too long ago—"

Lawrence pushes himself off the wall, his posture suddenly confrontational. "Why should we talk to you anyway? You don't have any authority."

"Actually, we do," I correct him, keeping my voice level. "We're Royal Investigators, appointed directly by the Duke to look into this matter." I reach into the pocket of my jacket where I keep placed my shiny new badge.

My fingers find nothing but lint and an old dog treat.

I pat my pocket more insistently, then check my other pockets. Nothing. The badge is gone.

"I swear I had it in my pocket," I say, a cold feeling settling in my stomach. "I put it there this morning."

Maggie gives me a questioning look, then understanding dawns on her face. "Your badge is missing?"

"It appears so," I say, trying to keep my voice steady while my mind races through possibilities. Did I leave it at the castle? Drop it somewhere in the village? Or— and this thought sends a chill through me— did someone *take* it?

Lawrence's expression shifts subtly, a flicker of something I can't quite read passing over his features.

"That's convenient," he says, his tone somewhere between mocking and suspicious.

Joe suddenly barks, the sound sharp in the morning air. He's staring at Lawrence intently, his posture alert but not aggressive.

"Looks like your dog is as confused about your authority as we are," Lawrence says with a smirk.

Pepper pulls against her handcuffs again, drawing our attention back to her. "Rebecca, I didn't do this," she says softly. "If you need help finding Luma, let me know."

"Of course," Maggie says smoothly. "We appreciate your time."

As we turn to leave, I feel Lawrence's eyes on my back. Joe stays close to my side, occasionally looking back over his shoulder.

"That was interesting," Maggie says quietly once we're out of earshot.

"Very," I agree. "Pepper seemed genuinely concerned about Luma."

"But Lawrence..."

"Lawrence was nervous," I finish for her. "And Joe noticed." I pat my empty pocket again, the missing badge weighing on my mind far more heavily than its physical presence ever did. "I need to retrace my steps, figure out when the badge disappeared."

"You think someone took it?" Maggie asks, her normally cheerful face serious.

"I think it's quite a coincidence that my badge goes missing while we're investigating a kidnapped dog," I reply. "And in my experience with both animals and people, there's rarely such a thing as coincidence."

Joe lets out a soft whine, looking back toward Lawrence, who still watches us from his position by the wall.

"I know, buddy," I tell him, scratching behind his ears. "I don't like him either."

THE STAFF DINING hall at Castle Atwood feels like a five-star restaurant. The scent of roasted garlic, fresh herbs, and something wonderfully savory that I can't quite place wafts through the busy room. Joe, ever the optimist when it comes to food, walks beside me with the dignified patience of a dog who knows dinner is imminent but is trying very hard to be sophisticated about it.

"Just remember your manners," I whisper to him as we approach the large oak doors. "No drooling."

Joe gives me a look that somehow manages to convey both deep offense and a solemn promise to behave himself.

Chef Renauld has outdone herself tonight. Vaulted ceilings with ornate moldings hover above walls paneled in rich mahogany. Candles cast a warm, golden glow over the long table that could easily seat thirty people but typically hosts only the core castle staff. The place settings gleam with what I'm pretty sure is actual silver, and the napkins are folded into complicated shapes that would put origami masters to shame.

"Rebecca! Joe! Over here!" Maggie waves enthusiastically from her seat near the middle of the table. "Saved you both a spot," Maggie says, patting the chair beside her and gesturing to a large cushion on the floor that's been set up for Joe. "Wait until you taste the beef bourguignon," Maggie leans in, her eyes sparkling.

"Oh, is *that* the special occasion?" I smirk, shaking my head. The dining hall is so over-decorated, I almost thought I'd forgotten it's a holiday, or someone's birthday. "The Chef is literally celebrating herself and what an incredible cook she is. She's made a holiday around her best meal."

"Can you blame her?" Maggie smirks. "Her beef bour- guignon *deserves* its own holiday."

The table is already set with baskets of fresh bread, small bowls of herb-infused olive oil, and carafes of water and wine. The bread looks crusty on the outside and pillow-soft on the inside, exactly the way bread should be.

"Is that from *Le Petit Scone*?" I ask, recognizing the distinc- tive braid pattern on one of the loaves.

"Henri's twisted braid!" Maggie confirms. "Chef Renauld and Henri seem to have reached a compromise. They were fighting last week over orders of flour, but it looks like they've mended the dispute."

As if summoned by her name, Chef Renauld emerges from the kitchen doors, pushing a cart laden with steaming dishes. Her white chef's coat is somehow immaculate despite what must have been hours of cooking, and her salt-and- pepper hair is tucked perfectly under her chef's hat. She moves with military precision, her back straight and her gaze sweeping the room like a general surveying her troops.

"*Mes amis*," she announces, her voice carrying the crisp authority of someone who expects— and receives— instant attention. "Tonight we have beef bourguignon with mush- rooms from our own gardens, roasted root vegetables with rosemary and thyme, and a wild rice pilaf with toasted almonds."

The room bursts into applause. Chef Renauld tries to look impassive under her hat, but I can tell that she's beaming with pride. Chef Renauld begins serving, assisted by two kitchen staff who move with the coordinated efficiency that speaks of her exacting standards. When she reaches us, she gives me a small nod that I've come to recognize as her version of a warm greeting.

"Miss Orange, I have prepared a portion for *Monsieur Joe* as well." She gestures to one of her assistants, who sets down a bowl for Joe containing what appears to be the same meal we're having, minus any ingredients that might be harmful to dogs. "I would never forget my favorite customer. Such a refined palate, he has."

Joe's nose twitches appreciatively, but true to his training, he remains seated, though I can feel the subtle vibration of his tail thumping against the floor.

"Okay, Joe— Wait—" I say, asking him to pause. Then, I let him loose. "Go eat!" Joe dives into the dish without a second glance.

Chef Renauld smiles at Joe, offering a wink of approval before making her way down the table. As Chef Renauld moves on, I notice Douglas enter the dining hall. The groundskeeper's weathered face is even more lined than usual, and there's a smudge of dirt across one cheek that he either hasn't noticed or hasn't bothered to wash off. His work clothes look like they've seen a hard day's labor, and his silver-streaked hair is sticking up at odd angles.

He drops heavily into a chair across from us, nodding a greeting that's more general than specific.

"Any luck today, Douglas?" Maggie asks, passing him the bread basket. She turns to me as if she's just remembered something. "Oh, Rebecca, I forgot to tell you— I asked Douglas to search the woods for any sign of Luma!"

My heart pounds in my chest, hoping for good news. But Douglas shakes his head.

"No luck," he replies, his Scottish brogue thickening with what I recognize as frustration. "Searched the North woods and the old stone walls by the lake. Not a trace of the collie."

"Oh," I say, setting down the bite of beef bourguignon that's perched on my fork. "We interviewed suspects in the village today. I'm afraid we haven't had much luck either." The heaviness of it all hits me, but I try not to melt under the feeling.

"We'll find the little lass," Douglas says, patting my shoulder. "Not to worry. The great Rebecca Orange has solved multiple cases in her time here. You won't fail now."

I hope not, I think, considering what failing might mean for the Duke and me. *Or Jack might never forgive me.*

"Just wish I had a better nose for Detective work," Douglas shrugs.

Then, it hits me. "What did you say?"

"I said—"

"A *nose* for it," I cut Douglas off. "You may not have the nose for it, but you know who does?" I glance down at Joe, who's already finished his dinner. His long nose is covered in grease, his tongue happy. "Douglas, you're a genius," I tell him.

"I know," Douglas agrees.

———

As soon as dinner is over, Joe and I rush back to my apartment.

"We're going to work tonight, buddy," I tell him, and his ears immediately perk up at the word "work." I'm fifty-three years old and talking to my dog like he understands every word— but that's the thing: after two decades together, he kind of does.

In the panic that followed Luma's absence, I didn't consider using Joe's nose to track her. But thankfully, it's not too late. I grab my tracking kit from the closet— a small backpack containing a flashlight, water bottle, first aid supplies for both humans and canines, treats for positive reinforcement, and a length of special tracking lead. Over twenty years working with animals has taught me to always be prepared. I clip a small red light to Joe's collar— just enough to keep eyes on him in the dark without ruining our night vision.

"Let's smell Luma's bed first," I say, letting Joe investigate the bed that's sitting in the corner. It's the last known place Luma was seen. "Sniff," I say, pointing at the bed. " Joe sniffs it from top to bottom. I give him time. You can't rush nature.

When he's done, he sits. I move to the doors that lead out into the garden, opening them wide. Then, I issue the command: "Find."

Joe leaps into action. His nose searches the ground, beginning to work the scent trail from Luma's bed outward. I attach his tracking lead— longer than a standard leash to give him room to work— and follow him as he leads me into the garden.

He works his way across the castle grounds, pulling me out into the crisp night air. Luma's scent won't be as strong now, but dogs can track movements even days after the original subject has disappeared. In fact, Joe's sense of smell is one hundred thousand times better than mine— which explains why it's so hard for him to resist a tasty treat. Dogs have *such* a good sense of smell that they can even detect cancer in humans and sniff out bombs.

I follow him across the grass, waiting as he pauses at a stone path. I stop to let Joe reorient himself. He circles twice, nose working overtime, then heads confidently toward the West side of the castle grounds. I follow, letting the lead hang loose between us, careful not to direct or influence his tracking.

"Good boy," I murmur as he maintains focus. "Find Luma."

The castle grounds are extensive, and Joe leads us past the formal gardens— silent and mysterious in the moonlight—

toward the edge of the manicured landscape where the more natural woodland begins. My breath catches in my throat.

This is where Luma's pawprints were found.

Now I know that Joe is absolutely on the right track. He leads me past the garden into the woods. The transition is gradual: perfectly trimmed hedges give way to more casually managed shrubbery, which eventually blends into the wild underbrush of the forest.

Joe doesn't hesitate at the forest's edge, plunging forward with the confidence of a tracker who's certain of his quarry's path. I click on my flashlight, keeping the beam low and slightly ahead of us to illuminate potential obstacles without disrupting Joe's concentration. We duck under a piece of the fence that's been cut since the day Luma went missing. My eyes scan the broken wire, imagining a person dressed in all black snapping the fence into pieces. A shiver runs down my spine. We're retracing the criminal's steps.

We push into the trees, leaving behind the official perimeter of the castle grounds and moving into public lands. The woods at night have a magical quality— slightly eerie but also peaceful. Moonlight filters through the canopy, creating dappled patterns on the forest floor. The sounds are different too: the soft hooting of an owl, the rustle of small nocturnal creatures, the whisper of leaves stirred by the gentle breeze.

I hate to think of Luma being led through to forest by whoever kidnapped her. The thought makes me shake with rage.

Whoever did this is going to pay.

Joe navigates through it all with single-minded determination, his nose leading us along a path that only he can perceive. We follow what seems to be a game trail for a while, then veer off into thicker underbrush. I have to duck under low-hanging branches and step carefully over exposed roots, but Joe moves with surprising agility for his size, never losing the scent.

"You've got it, buddy," I encourage softly. "Keep going."

After about twenty minutes of trekking through the woods, the trees begin to thin, and I can see lights ahead— the Village of Atwood. Joe's pace quickens slightly, suggesting the scent is getting stronger. We emerge from the forest at the edge of the village, and it hits me:

Someone took Luma all the way to the village.

Could she be in someone's home? Or hidden in the back of a shop? Wherever she is, she's not getting much exercise. We've put posters all over the village. If she'd been taken for a walk, someone would have called it in.

Joe leads me onto a cobblestone path. We're away from the town square in a more residential section of Atwood. At this hour, most windows are dark, though a few still glow with warm light. The cobblestone streets gleam faintly in the moonlight, and the pastel-colored buildings look silver and blue in the night's palette.

Joe turns right, leading us along the village's perimeter rather than into its center. We're at Atwood's outer edge. The trail leads us to a row of small cottages set slightly apart from the main village. They're charming structures— older, and less popular among locals— with stone foundations and timber frames.

Then, abruptly, Joe stops. He whines. He circles, then looks up at me with a confused expression I've seen only rarely in our tracking work.

"Lost the trail?" I ask, though I already know the answer.

Joe circles once more, checking in all directions, but his body language is clear: the scent ends here. His head hangs low. He knows we were trying to find Luma. And it breaks his heart that he can't go any further.

I kneel beside him, stroking his thick fur. "Good boy, Joe. You did great." I reward him with a treat from my pack, which he accepts with dignity but without his usual enthusiasm.

I study the cottages. This is an older part of Atwood, and the housing is cheaper here than in the village square. The homes are modest but well-maintained, with flower boxes under the windows and a small stone path leading to the door.

Luma could be in one of these houses.

I check my watch— it's nearly midnight. Too late to knock on doors and ask questions without seeming like a threat.

"Well, Joe," I say quietly, "we've narrowed it down. That's progress."

I take out my phone and snap a few photos of the cottages. I also drop a pin on my map app to mark the exact location where we stopped.

"Time to head back," I tell Joe, who looks at the cottage one more time before reluctantly turning away from the unfinished trail. "Don't worry— we'll find her."

Joe walks beside me, still in his professional mode but more relaxed now that we've paused the active tracking. His GPS on his collar blinks steadily as we make our way back toward Castle Atwood, whose illuminated towers are visible even from the village.

"Don't worry, Joe," I promise, both to him and to myself. "She's still out there." I say the words, even though I'm not sure I totally believe them.

THE NEXT DAY, Maggie, Joe, and I gather at the Royal Investigators office to strategize. The morning light streams through the office's windows, casting long rectangles of sunshine over our collection of evidence. Joe stretches out beneath the desk, his massive body somehow fitting into a space that should be too small for him, his golden coat catching the light. I've been awake since five a.m., my mind churning with theories about who kidnapped Luma and why.

"OK, let's go through it again," Maggie says, her blonde braids catching the light as she leans forward. "Last night, Joe led you to the cottages—"

"But he couldn't figure out which one," I confirm.

"Those cottages are older," Maggie thinks aloud. "I see them for rent all the time. That area has vacancies because the cottages aren't remodeled— they're prone to plumbing problems and safety issues. And most people would rather choose a new apartment in the middle of town. The cottages are a bit of a walk from the center of Atwood— twenty minutes, at least." Maggie taps her chin, considering. "Is it possible someone hid Luma in one of the vacant cottages that's for rent?"

"That could be," I say, nodding eagerly. "Maybe they're keeping her there until they can move her somewhere else without getting caught? They might have rented it out just for this purpose…"

"The cottages are cheap," Maggie agrees. "If I were going to rent a place to hide a dog, I'd pick something inexpensive. We should check with a local real estate agent and see if any cottages have been rented in the last month."

"Great idea!" I say, feeling like we're really getting somewhere.

Maggie leans across her desk, pushing a few printed pages at me. "I did some digging on our friend Lawrence last night."

"And?"

"Turns out he owes money after a car accident. Public records show a court case. He slammed into someone while driving recklessly. T-boned the poor lady. He owes her thousands of dollars."

"That's a heavy price tag for someone who claims to abstain from capitalism," I say, letting out a low whistle. "Has he paid her back yet?"

"I made a call," Maggie smiles at me. "And the woman was happy to share with me that he has *not*, in fact, paid her back. She's thinking of asking the county to garnish his wages, if there are any."

"So that's a possible motive," I say, nodding. "Maybe he stole Luma hoping to get a ransom?"

It's an idea I want to explore further, but just then, the door to our office flies open without a knock, smothering my good mood. Joe jumps to his feet— his posture alert but not aggressive— as Officer Basilier storms in. She's in her full uniform, her short, powerful frame somehow making the room feel smaller. Her eyes scan our evidence board with barely disguised contempt.

"Officer Basilier," Maggie says, switching instantly to her professional voice. "What can we do for you this morning?"

"You can come with me," Basilier says. It's not a request. Her hand rests on her belt, uncomfortably close to her handcuffs. "Both of you. Now."

"Let me guess," I stand up. "You're inviting us to breakfast? I'm not one to turn down a waffle. What about you, Joe?" Joe moves to my side, his massive body a comforting presence against my leg.

"Your jokes are getting old, Miss Orange. But you won't be laughing soon enough." A thin, satisfied smile crosses her face. "Come with me. Bring the dog if you must."

Maggie and I exchange a glance. This can't be good.

"Should we call the Duke?" Maggie whispers as we follow Basilier out onto the street. The office door shuts behind us with an ominous clang. My feet click against the cobblestone as we follow Officer Basilier past charming pastel buildings, ivy weaving up the exterior walls.

"Not yet," I murmur back. "Let's see what this is about first."

Besides, the Duke has enough on his plate right now. Like his uncle dying and the woman he's dating losing his dog.

Officer Basilier marches us down the road. She glances over her shoulder as we follow her. "Try anything and I'll add resisting arrest to the charges."

Charges? My stomach clenches. What charges?

"Me? Try something?" I say, throwing my hands in the air. "I'm just a woman hoping for a waffle. No funny business here."

Officer Basilier rolls her eyes and flips her head back around, marching us down the street. Normally, I enjoy walking the cobblestone streets of Atwood Village. Today, each step feels like walking toward a trap.

Great. I'm out for a casual stroll with my mortal enemy.

"What do you think this is about?" Maggie whispers as we follow several paces behind Officer Basilier.

"No idea," I whisper back. "But she seems... happy. That doesn't bode well for us."

Joe stays close to my side, his usual exploratory sniffing abandoned in favor of protective vigilance. Smart dog. He knows something's wrong.

The Tourism Board office appears on the corner. As we approach, I notice a small crowd has gathered outside. The door is blocked with police tape, and even from a distance, I can see something isn't right. The large front window has been shattered, glass scattered across the sidewalk like diamonds in the morning sun.

"Make way," Officer Basilier commands, and the crowd parts reluctantly, revealing more of the damage.

My breath catches in my throat. The office— normally a pristine showcase of Monrovian charm with its neat displays of brochures and tasteful exhibition of local crafts— has been destroyed. Completely, utterly destroyed.

Display racks lie toppled and broken. Brochures litter the floor like oversized confetti. The beautiful scale model of Castle Atwood that once greeted visitors has been smashed, tiny stone towers and miniature flags crushed underfoot. But worst of all are the walls. Someone has spray-painted crude messages across the cream-colored surface:

True Monrovians Only!

Royals are for Monrovians, not tourists!

Tourists go home!

"Oh my God," Maggie breathes beside me. "This is hateful. And kind of manic."

Officer Basilier turns to face us, her expression triumphant. "Happened sometime last night. A complete destruction of public property. Estimated damages over fifty thousand euros."

"That's awful," I say, genuinely disturbed. "But why bring us here?"

"Because of this." Basilier signals to one of her junior officers, who approaches with a clear evidence bag. Inside is a small, metallic object that catches the light.

My Royal Investigator badge.

Its gold surface gleams back at me, my own name etched on the bottom. I remember the day Maggie had the badges made as a symbol of our official titles. Now, our pride has come to bite us.

"Where did you find that?" I ask, my voice suddenly hoarse.

"Right in the middle of the crime scene," Basilier says, her voice dripping with satisfaction.

"Now, hold on," I say. "The badge is mine, but—"

"We know it's yours," Basilier interrupts. "And we have a witness who saw someone matching your description wandering around the village late at night."

"That could have been anyone!" Maggie says.

"The witness described," Officer Basilier checks her notes, "an incredibly average looking woman accompanied by a dog the size of a horse loitering around the cottages well past midnight."

"Well now we *know* it's not me," I quip. "I'm exceptionally good-looking, not average. There must be another, less-attractive woman with a big dog and insomnia wandering around town."

Officer Basilier rolls her eyes. "Then may I ask… what *were* you doing last night?"

"I was…" I pause. "I was wandering around the village with Joe. But we were looking for Luma! Her scent led him to the cottages. We weren't anywhere near the tourism office. You can ask Maggie. I was just filling her in on what we learned…"

"Ms. Lefevere can hardly provide an alibi when she's likely your accomplice," Basilier says, turning her gaze to Maggie. "After all, you both had reason to want to sabotage the Tourism Board's work."

"What reason would we possibly have?" Maggie asks, her voice steady despite the absurdity of the accusation. "I've been helping the board plan the upcoming *'Day of Love'* event!"

"Exactly," Officer Basilier says, nodding. "The two of you are overworked. Look at how many jobs you have. Animal trainer. Royal Investigator. And you, Maggie! Head of House-hold. Member of the tourism board. Amateur Detective…"

"What, now it's a crime to have *hobbies?*" I snort. "A few of the villagers play checkers by the fountain on Saturdays! Guess you'd better arrest them, too!"

"You are disgruntled employees," Officer Basilier says, pointing a finger at me. "You were angry that the Duke had delegated so much work to you…"

"Guess she doesn't know how often we stop for lavender lattes," Maggie whispers to me under her breath. "Joke's on her, we hardly work at all."

"… and you admire the Royal Family and abhor the idea of outsiders such as tourists invading the Village of Atwood!"

"That's not true! We love tourists—"

Officer Basilier cuts me off. "So you broke into the tourism office and sent a message as a warning! Perhaps you're also responsible for the disappearance of Luma," she adds. "After all, the dog was last seen in your care."

My mind is racing. This isn't just an accusation— it's a setup. Someone has deliberately planted my things at the crime scene. Someone wants to frame me for vandalism, and possibly for Luma's kidnapping as well.

"Rebecca had nothing to do with this," Maggie says, shaking her head. "In fact, it has Pepper and Lawrence written all over it! They got in a spat with the tourism office just the other day…"

"Maggie's right. This is ridiculous," I agree, trying to keep my voice level. "Why would I leave my badge at a crime scene?"

"Perhaps you're not as clever as you think you are," Basilier says with a shrug. "Criminals often make mistakes."

Joe lets out a low growl, sensing my distress. I place a steadying hand on his massive head, feeling his warmth seep into my palm.

"Officer Basilier," Maggie says in her most diplomatic voice, "Surely you can see this doesn't make sense. Rebecca has been supporting village committees since she moved to Monrovia. And she's trying to find the Duke's missing dog. Why would she do something that would only distract from the case?"

"Because you were getting nowhere," Basilier says. "And your precious Duke needed results. So you decided to create a distraction. Make it look like some anti-royalist vandal was responsible for both crimes."

"That's not—"

"Or perhaps," she continues. "You were seeking revenge. Andre, a member of the board, told us you were quite angry after one of your dogs attacked him. Perhaps you held a grudge."

"He's the only one who held a grudge!" Maggie exclaims.

Actually, I think, *I've absolutely held a grudge against him since that moment, and probably always will.* But I know better than to admit such a stupid thing out loud.

I stare at the devastation inside the Tourism Board office, and suddenly I understand. I'm being framed by someone who wants to stop me from finding Luma. Which means we must be getting close.

"Officer Basilier," I say carefully, "I think someone is setting me up precisely *because* Maggie and I are close to solving Luma's kidnapping. Have you considered that?"

"What I've considered," Basilier says, stepping closer, "is that you arrived in our country only recently and have since inserted yourself into royal affairs, appointed yourself a detective without any credentials, and now a dog is missing and a government office destroyed."

"That's not fair," Maggie protests. "Rebecca has done nothing but help since she arrived."

"Help whom? The Duke? The Royal Family that believes they're above the law?" Basilier's voice rises. "Well, not anymore."

She reaches into her belt and produces a pair of handcuffs that gleam in the morning sunlight. The crowd around us has grown, and I recognize faces from the village— Henri from *Le Petit Scone* watching with a concerned expression, Benjamin from the pet shop filming with his phone, tourists pausing mid-photo to stare at the unfolding drama. Jocelyn, the owner of *Cafe de Flore,* is in the crowd, bouncing nervously on her heels as she looks at the scene.

My heart is pounding so hard I'm sure everyone can hear it. This can't be happening. I came to Monrovia for a fresh start, to work with animals in a beautiful castle, not to be arrested for crimes I didn't commit.

Officer Basilier holds out the handcuffs, her expression a mixture of triumph and disdain.

"I'm very pleased to finally announce that you, Ms. Rebecca Orange, are under arrest."

Joe lets out a long, plaintive whine, pressing his body against my legs as if to shield me from what's coming next.

CHAPTER
Twelve

THE INK FEELS cold and slightly sticky against my fingertips as Officer Basilier presses each one methodically onto the fingerprint card. All I've tried to do since I arrived in Monrovia is be a force for good. Now, here I am, being processed like a common criminal while my 250-pound Tibetan Mastiff whines softly from where he's tethered to a nearby bench.

"Maggie," I say, my face deadpan. I try to make a joke to take the edge off my fear. "When I agreed to move to Monrovia for the job, this wasn't mentioned in the welcome packet."

"Don't worry, Rebecca!" Maggie calls to me over the counter, her tone frantic. "Everything's going to be okay!"

"It feels okay!" I shout back, cringing as one of my fingers brushes up against a piece of paper.

"Press harder," Officer Basilier commands, her grip tightening around my wrist. She's surprisingly strong for someone so petite.

I comply, pressing my index finger firmly against the paper. "I haven't finger-painted in a while," I say, forcing a smile. "Maybe next we'll break out the crayons?"

"Glad you still have your sense of humor." Officer Basilier's tone is flat, unimpressed. She's cold and empty— just like the Police Station that surrounds us.

"This is completely unnecessary," Maggie declares from where she stands in the lobby. Her normally impeccable blonde braids are slightly disheveled, and she looks a mess. From the moment Officer Basilier hauled me away, she's been on the phone, trying to intervene. "I've already put a call into the Duke, and there's going to be hell to pay when—"

Officer Basilier doesn't even look up from my fingerprints. "The law applies to everyone, Ms. Lefevere. Even those employed by your precious Duke."

"It's standard procedure," I tell Maggie, trying to sound more confident than I feel. "Don't worry, this is fun. It's just like the TV shows I watch. I'm pretending I'm on a crime show."

"Crime shows," Officer Basilier mutters with a snort. "This isn't television, Ms. Orange. This is a real investigation into a real crime."

"A crime I didn't commit," I remind her, wincing as she presses my thumb down with extra force.

Joe makes a low, rumbling sound from his bench. He can sense my rising anxiety. I shoot him a reassuring look, but his amber eyes remain fixed on Officer Basilier, tracking her every movement like she's a predator he needs to monitor.

"That's for the courts to decide," Officer Basilier says, finally releasing my hand. She picks up the fingerprint card and examines it with critical eyes.

From the waiting area, a woman's voice rises above the ambient noise. "This is exactly how it starts! First, they criminalize the castle staff, next they'll be coming for the rest of us!"

I turn my head to see Pepper, standing on one of the waiting room chairs. She's dressed entirely in black and red, with fishnet sleeves covering her arms and dark makeup emphasizing her fierce expression.

Oh my gosh, I think, feeling my body flood with relief. *I never thought I'd be so happy to see Pepper.*

Her boyfriend, Lawrence, stands beside her, dressed in punk clothing and looking both embarrassed and supportive.

"Pepper, please get down from there," Maggie says with the weary tone of someone who has had this conversation many times before.

"We will not be silenced!" Pepper continues, ignoring Maggie completely. "The people stand with the falsely accused!"

Lawrence nods along, though his enthusiasm seems more manufactured than genuine. "Yeah, what she said."

"Good work, Pepper!" I shout at her. "Keep making trouble. I've never been so happy to see you in my life." Officer Basilier moves across the counter to collect some paperwork, giving me a chance to mutter to Maggie. "I didn't realize I had supporters."

Maggie sighs, her tone annoyed and urgent. "You don't, not really. Pepper and Lawrence will protest anything."

"At least they're consistent," I say.

"We can hear you," Pepper shouts. "But I'm still on your side because this is tyranny!"

"Yeah!" Lawrence agrees.

"You're arresting the wrong person!" Pepper adds.

"Yeah!" Lawrence says again.

"If anything, you should be arresting *us!*"

"Yea— wait," Lawrence pauses. "Why would you say that?"

"Because," Pepper shrugs. "Isn't it obvious? This is totally the kind of crime I would commit. It matches my behavior almost perfectly. It's protesting a cause. It's visible and public to get attention." Pepper pauses, lost in thought and chewing on an idea. "Actually, it's weird how similar this is to something I would do. Isn't it strange? It's almost as if someone was inspired by me..."

Officer Basilier returns, slapping a form down in front of me. "Sign here, acknowledging that you understand the charges against you."

I scan the document, my stomach tightening as I read: "Interfering with a police investigation and destruction of public property." The words swim before my eyes, making the situation feel suddenly more real, more serious.

"This is absurd," Maggie interjects, stepping closer to the desk. "The Duke will get these charges dismissed as soon as he's back in town. All Rebecca's been doing is her job!"

"Her job is to take care of animals at the castle," Officer Basilier counters, her voice hardening. "Not to play detective in an active investigation."

"The Duke specifically asked for her assistance," Maggie argues, her professional demeanor slipping to reveal genuine anger. "You're overstepping, Officer! I'll see to it you get what's coming to you!"

"You will?" Officer Basilier turns to face Maggie fully, her stance widening slightly as if preparing for confrontation. "Because last I checked, Rebecca's personal property was found at the scene of a crime. That's a fact."

"The facts," Maggie says, stepping closer, "are that you've had it out for the castle ever since the Duke opened it to the public. And this little power play might cost you your job."

From his bench, Joe gives a low woof that sounds suspiciously like agreement.

"Is that a threat, Ms. Lefevere?" Officer Basilier asks, her voice eerily calm.

"It's a reality check," Maggie replies. "Rebecca is here because she's good at her job— so good that she noticed something you missed. And instead of being grateful for the assistance, you're throwing her in jail."

Officer Basilier collects my signed form, her movements deliberately slow. "I'm enforcing the law. Something the Royal

Family seems to think doesn't apply to them or their employees."

"You have no right to hold her!" Maggie shouts across the counter. "Bail has already been posted—"

"Yes," Officer Basilier agrees, "But sadly, Rebecca has to wait in a holding cell while we process all the paperwork. And I'm feeling quite slow with my typing lately. I might not even get to it until tomorrow morning…"

"Down with the systemic abuse of power!" Pepper shouts from the waiting area, now standing on a different chair. "Justice for castle workers!"

"Yeah!" Lawrence adds, pumping his fist with halfhearted enthusiasm even though he doesn't seem to understand what Pepper means. "What she said!"

I catch Maggie's eye and mouth "thank you," genuinely touched by her fierce defense. She gives me a quick smile before turning back to Officer Basilier.

"Process her if you must," Maggie says, "but know that this isn't over. The Duke values loyalty above almost everything else. You've messed with someone he cares about, and he's going to see you fired for it. And if the Duke can't make this right, I promise you…" Maggie's eyes darken. "I will."

Officer Basilier's jaw tightens, but she maintains her professional demeanor. "Fingerprinting is complete. Now for the mug shot."

She guides me to a height chart on the wall, positioning me with clinical detachment. "Face forward. No smiling."

I stare straight ahead, trying to maintain my dignity as the camera clicks. Joe whines again, more urgently this time.

"It's okay, buddy," I call to him, but he's getting more agitated, shifting his massive weight from paw to paw.

Officer Basilier takes another photo, this time of my profile, before leading me back toward the desk. "Personal effects," she says, pushing a small plastic bin toward me.

I remove my watch and the castle key card hanging

around my neck, placing them in the container. Each item feels like another piece of my freedom being stripped away.

"Hold on," I say as I finish. "What about Joe? Who's going to take care of him while I'm in here?"

Officer Basilier glances at the massive dog with thinly veiled disdain. "That's not my concern. Ms. Lefevere can take him back to the castle."

Joe's ears prick up at this, and he rises to his full height, his eyes locked on Officer Basilier.

"That won't work," I say quickly. "Joe's trained to stay with me. He gets... anxious when we're separated."

"Anxious?" Officer Basilier repeats flatly.

"He's a therapy animal," I improvise, stretching the truth. I don't mention he's only a therapy animal in the sense that his bad behavior made me *need* therapy.

"He's the worst-behaved therapy animal I've ever seen," Officer Basilier counters.

"He's actually a Tibetan Mastiff, and they come with special abilities," I correct her, unable to help myself. I don't mention that his special ability is eating more cheese even after he's bloated himself to fullness. "And he's extremely gentle unless he feels I'm being threatened."

As if on cue, Joe lets out a low, rumbling growl. It starts deep in his chest, a sound more felt than heard, before gradually rising in volume. His hackles rise, transforming his usually fluffy appearance into something more primeval.

Officer Basilier's hand instinctively moves toward her weapon. "Control your animal, Ms. Orange."

"I am controlling him," I say calmly. "He's still sitting, isn't he? But if you separate us, I can't guarantee he'll stay this composed."

Joe rises slowly to his feet, the full majesty of his size now apparent. His golden coat seems to bristle with electricity, and the rumble in his chest deepens. He doesn't lunge or bark—

he doesn't need to. His message is clear without those theatrics.

"Listen to her, Officer," Maggie advises, keeping her distance from Joe. "That dog once tore through a solid oak door when someone accidentally locked Rebecca in a supply closet. Imagine what he might do to cell bars."

This is a complete fabrication— Joe has never destroyed anything more substantial than a tennis ball— but Officer Basilier doesn't know that.

Pepper, standing on a chair and pumping a fist in the air, adds, "Denying an innocent woman her therapy animal is cruelty! We demand humane treatment!"

"Yeah!" Lawrence echoes, seeming slightly more invested now that there's a massive dog involved. "Animal rights!"

Officer Basilier surveys the scene— the increasingly agitated dog, the protesting anarchists, the determined castle administrator— and I can see her calculating whether this particular battle is worth fighting.

"Fine," she finally concedes, though her tone suggests this is far from over. "The dog can stay with you. But if he causes any trouble, any trouble at all, he's out. And that's on you, Ms. Orange."

"He'll be a perfect gentleman," I promise, relief washing over me. "Joe, heel."

Immediately, Joe's demeanor changes. The growling stops, his hackles lower, and he trots over to me with the innocence of a puppy. I scratch behind his ears, murmuring quiet praise for his performance.

"This way," Officer Basilier says, gesturing toward the hallway that leads to the cells. "Your accommodations await."

I pat my thigh, signaling Joe to follow, and together we trail after Officer Basilier. The hallway is narrow, forcing Joe to walk behind me rather than at my side. His warm breath against my hand is immensely comforting.

"I'll be back!" Maggie calls after us. "Don't worry, Rebecca!"

"And we'll keep the protest going outside!" Pepper adds. "The people united will never be defeated!"

"The people are undefeatable!" Lawrence's voice follows us down the hall.

The cell area is small, with just three holding cells in total. Officer Basilier unlocks the middle cell and stands aside.

"Home sweet home," she says with no trace of humor. "Dinner is at six."

I step inside, Joe following closely. The cell is basic but clean— a narrow cot, a stainless steel toilet partially obscured by a low partition, and a small sink. The bars are solid and freshly painted.

Officer Basilier locks the door behind us, the metallic clang echoing through the empty room. "Enjoy your stay, Ms. Orange."

Once she's gone, I sink onto the cot, the reality of my situation finally hitting me full force. Joe immediately presses his massive body against my legs, resting his head in my lap.

"Well, this is a first," I tell him, running my fingers through his thick fur. "Twenty years of working with dangerous animals, and I get arrested for being too nosy. I always thought for sure I'd get arrested because you broke into a bakery or drug me into a bank vault, but this is all my own doing. Ironic, isn't it?"

Joe whines softly, his amber eyes fixed on my face with unmistakable concern.

"Don't worry," I assure him, though my confidence feels hollow. "Jack and Maggie will sort this out. We just have to get through tonight."

I shift on the uncomfortable cot, trying to find a position that might allow for sleep later. Joe settles onto the floor beside me, his body taking up nearly half the available space in the cell.

"At least I'm not alone," I whisper, leaning down to press my face against his fur. He smells like home— like the castle gardens and the special shampoo I use on him, with underlying notes of the treats I keep in my pockets. "Thank you for being here, Joe."

He lets out a deep sigh and sinks into the mattress. That's the special thing about animals. They'd rather be *with* you in prison than alone in a castle. Not many people can promise a woman the same.

Outside, I can faintly hear Pepper's voice leading what sounds like the beginning of a protest chant. Despite everything, this makes me smile. It's nice to have supporters, even if they're only supporting me because it gives them something to protest. I quietly wonder whether or not Pepper was responsible for vandalizing the tourism board. She was right when she said it follows her pattern of protest. But I truly believe Pepper would have owned up to what she did rather than watch me get locked up. And if she didn't do it, who did? There's Lawrence, but I can't imagine what his motivation would be.

Unless he knows I'm close to figuring out who stole Luma, and he wants to stop me because it's him, I think. Maggie's revelation about Lawrence needing to pay back a debt makes him an even more likely suspect.

The pieces of the case swim in my mind. I lean back against the wall, Joe's warmth against my legs, and I can't help but think— it's going to be a very long stay.

CHAPTER
Thirteen

A FEW HOURS LATER, and the metallic sound of a key sliding into a lock makes me jump. Joe's head snaps up, his ears perked forward in alert attention. I hear the main door to the holding area open, followed by footsteps— one set brisk and light, another heavier and determined.

"As I said, Your Grace, this is highly irregular. We have procedures that must be followed, and Ms. Orange has compromised a sensitive—"

"What's irregular, Officer Basilier, is arresting a member of the castle staff without bothering to inform me." The Duke's voice cuts through Officer Basilier's protests like a hot knife through butter. My heart leaps at the sound. "Worse yet, you've arrested the girlfriend of a member of the Royal Family without so much as a phone call."

Girlfriend? I think, trying not to get carried away. *Jack's never called me his girlfriend before.*

They appear in front of my cell— Officer Basilier standing rigidly, keys clutched in her hand, and beside her, the Duke of Atwood, looking like thunder in human form. His salt-and-pepper hair is slightly disheveled, as if he rushed here straight from bed, but his eyes are sharp and focused. He's wearing a casual sweater and jeans rather than his usual tailored attire, another sign of his haste.

"Rebecca." My name on his lips sounds like both a question and a relief. "I came as quickly as I could. Are you alright? Are you—"

"Did you bring any snacks?" I ask, grinning. "I'd like a cheeseburger."

Jack seems to visibly relax at the sight of me. He notices Joe at my heel, his tail wagging at the sight of the Duke.

"Joe got arrested, too?" Jack laughs, surprised. "What was his crime?"

"Being too adorable," I say gravely. "The most egregious of offenses."

Behind Jack's shoulder, Officer Basilier shifts her weight side to side, looking nervous and maybe— just maybe— humbled. She adds eagerly, "We normally wouldn't allow animals, but we wanted Rebecca to have her therapy dog with her. To be comfortable…" Her body language tells me she's just realized she made a huge mistake.

That's right, I think. *It's only just hitting you that this will cost you your job.*

"Open the cell," the Duke commands, not looking at Officer Basilier.

She hesitates, her knuckles whitening around the keys. "Before we remedy this situation, I just want to say that everything was done to the letter. We have evidence that ties Miss Orange to the scene of a crime—"

"I said open it." His voice doesn't rise, but the temperature in the room seems to drop by several degrees. "Or perhaps my aunt— the Queen— would be interested to hear how you've treated a guest of the Royal Family. She's grown quite fond of Miss Orange after learning how happy she makes me. She's also grieving the loss of my uncle— the King— and will be enraged to hear that I've missed his funeral because of your incompetence."

Officer Basilier's face tightens, but she steps forward and unlocks the cell door. The metal hinges groan as it swings open, and I don't wait for a formal invitation. I walk out with as much dignity as I can muster in yesterday's rumpled clothes, Joe padding faithfully by my side.

As soon as I clear the threshold, any pretense of restraint evaporates. I practically run the three steps into the Duke's arms. His embrace is solid and warm, his arms wrapping around me with surprising strength. I hadn't realized how scared I'd been until this moment of safety, and something inside me cracks.

"I've got you," he murmurs into my hair, and then, in a move that takes my breath away, he tilts my face up and kisses me.

It's brief but unmistakable— his lips warm against mine, a gesture that crosses the line from friendly comfort into something altogether different. When he pulls back, there's a flash of vulnerability in his eyes. It's as if he thought he'd lost me.

Officer Basilier clears her throat loudly. "If you're quite finished, there's paperwork to be processed for her release."

The Duke turns to her, keeping one arm firmly around my shoulders. "There will be no paperwork because there should have been no arrest. Rebecca Orange is here at my personal invitation for two purposes: first, to oversee the care of the castle's animals, and second, to serve as a Royal Investigator. Whatever she was doing, she had my implicit permission to engage in the matter."

"She left her badge at the scene of a crime! Surely you're not suggesting you approved the destruction of the tourism board offices?"

"If I did, it would be *me* you might charge, given that Rebecca is obligated by Monrovian law to follow my orders," Jack says, his voice hard as granite. "And since when does circumstantial evidence warrant a jail stay without so much as a trial? In truth, this isn't new, is it?" The Duke steps forward, casting a long shadow across the hallway. "I should have had you fired when you locked *me* up in a cell without evidence. I thought I was being noble. I wrote your incompetence off as hate for the Royals, which I could easily dismiss. But this goes much further. You, Officer Basilier, are a threat to every Monrovian."

Officer Basilier's eyes widen in horror. She looks as if he's hit her over the head with a frying pan.

That's right, I think, smiling to myself, *you're about to lose your job!*

"We've been investigating the disappearance of the dog," Officer Basilier says desperately. "You'll be pleased with our progress. You're going to want to see the evidence we have before you make any rash decisions."

"No, thank you," the Duke counters. "I've learned not to expect much from the Police in such matters. Besides, I've got my own Royal Investigators on the case of Luma's disappearance. Now, I'm taking Ms. Orange with me. If you have further questions for her, you can direct them through my office, where she will be happy to cooperate with a properly conducted investigation."

I can't help the small, satisfied smile that forms on my lips. Officer Basilier catches it and narrows her eyes.

"This isn't over," she says quietly.

"On that, we agree," the Duke replies. He guides me toward the door, Joe following close behind. "Oh, and Officer? The King and Queen are quite angry at the situation. Their lawyers are looking at the most prudent ways to assure your dismissal."

Her face pales slightly. "The monarchy has no direct authority over police appointments. That would be a parliamentary matter."

"True," the Duke concedes with a cold smile. "But you'd be surprised how many members of Parliament enjoy the Royal

Family's frequent hospitality. I wouldn't count on your job security just yet."

"I thought you didn't use your royal station for special treatment!" Officer Basilier says.

The Duke looks at me. "When it comes to the people I care about, I'll do anything necessary to ensure their well-being. Good day, Officer."

With Joe trotting behind us, Jack leads me through a short corridor and into a small office area where a desk sergeant quickly averts his eyes, suddenly fascinated by paperwork. My few belongings— phone, wallet, and the small notebook I'd been using to track my findings about Luma— are returned to me in a plastic bag.

Once we're in the empty lobby, Jack's composed facade cracks slightly. "Are you all right? Did they treat you decently?" His eyes scan me for injuries, his brow furrowed with concern.

"I'm fine," I assure him, touched by his worry. "Just tired and hungry. The accommodations weren't exactly five-star."

His expression darkens. "This is unacceptable. Basilier has been difficult before, but this crosses a line. She's using you to get at me."

"What do you mean?"

"It's a provocation," he explains. "And possibly a distraction from whatever's really happening with Luma and the other incidents at the castle. I am so sorry to have tangled you up in this, Rebecca."

I think about this for a moment. "Maggie and I have Officer Basilier on our list of suspects in Luma's disappearance."

Jack scratches his chin. "If you'd told me that a week ago I would have questioned it. But now— after what she's done—"

"I know," I agree. "Maybe Officer Basilier framed me because she's desperate to stop us from discovering who took

Luma. She hates that we opened the Royal Investigators office. Before Luma went missing she was threatening us with permit violations and fines. Maybe she lost control and took the dog to try and create a case she could solve instead of us? To show everyone the Atwood Police are still worthwhile."

"But why not return Luma?" Jack asks. "Wouldn't she have pretended to have found her by now?"

"I don't know," I shrug. "Maybe she got in too deep and now she's afraid to pretend to 'find' Luma because it will bring too much scrutiny." I pause, thinking over the ramifications of my theory. "Officer Basilier is just one suspect. Don't worry. We haven't given up looking for Luma. We're going to find her, Jack."

Jack raises an eyebrow, a smile crossing his face. "Getting framed for a crime hasn't scared you off the case?"

"Of course not!" I say, aghast. "I can't let her down. I think of the poor dog out there all on her own or with some maniac, and I know it's all my fault—" For the first time, tears threaten to spill down my cheeks. It takes everything I have to hold it together. "And to top it off, I've let *you* down."

"You could never let me down," Jack says, the earnestness in his tone telling me he means it. "We'll find Luma. I told you— I picked a scrappy dog for a reason. Wherever she is, I know she's giving them hell. She might just find her way back to us before we find *her*. Wouldn't that be something?"

Beside me, Joe lets out a mournful whine. Jack reaches down and scratches his ears.

"Let's go. I'll take you to *Cafe de Flore* for your first meal as a free woman." His expression softens, the corner of his mouth lifting in a half-smile that does interesting things to my pulse rate. "You must be starving."

"That sounds wonderful," I say, suddenly aware of just how hungry I am. "Though I probably look like a disaster."

"You look perfect," he says simply, and the warmth in his eyes makes me believe him, rumpled clothes and all. "There's just one complication," the Duke adds, glancing toward the front of the station. "Word of your arrest seems to have leaked to the press. There are photographers out front."

I groan. "Fantastic. Just what I need— my jail mugshot splashed across Monrovian tabloids."

"They won't get the chance," he promises. "We'll go out the back way. I have a car waiting."

He peers out a small window, then gestures for us to follow. "Ready for a bit of royal escape artistry?"

Despite everything, I find myself smiling. "Lead the way, Your Grace."

Jack cringes at my joking use of his title. Joe barks in agreement as Jack offers me his hand, and I take it without hesitation. With Joe at our heels, we slip through a service door and into the bright morning sunshine, leaving Officer Basilier and her jail cell behind us. For now, at least, I'm free— and with the two companions I'd choose above all others.

Fourteen

LATER, I'm home, and it feels good to be back. The dusty, familiar scent of Castle Atwood wraps around me like a blanket, but my return feels surreal. The stone corridors seem to wind around me in unfamiliar patterns. Maybe it's because I was in a jail cell this morning, or maybe it's because Joe keeps looking at me like I might disappear again. Either way, as I walk through the East wing, following Maggie's brisk pace, I can't help but feel like I've stepped into someone else's life. Twenty-four hours ago, I was being fingerprinted. Now I'm back at work as if nothing happened.

"I still can't believe she actually arrested you," Maggie says, her tablet clutched to her chest like a shield. "Over your badge being placed there, no less. Clearly someone was trying to frame you…"

Beside us, Joe's massive paws click against the polished stone floor. He offers a soft woof in agreement.

"I thought the same thing," I say. "In some ways, I'm honored they'd try to frame me. It's like I have a fan or something."

"More like a stalker. You got your badge back, right?"

I remove the Royal Investigator badge from my pocket,

holding it up for her to see. "Officer Basilier tried to claim she had to keep it as evidence, but Jack was able to intervene by order of Royal decree so I could have it back."

"Royal decrees are usually for Dukes and Duchesses," Maggie grins. "Not badges."

I polish the badge on the edge of my shirt, trying to rub off the memories of where it's been. "Still, it's as good as new. And— Maggie— I was thinking about the day it went missing. It *had* to have been one of the suspects we interviewed who stole it."

We turn a corner, and sunlight streams through tall windows, illuminating motes of dust in the air.

"The important thing," Maggie continues, lowering her voice, "is that you're out now. And you should have heard Jack when I called him. He dropped everything, Rebecca. Everything."

"He's just an amazing guy," I say, trying to keep my tone light. "He did it because he has good character. He's chivalrous."

"*Rebecca*," Maggie says emphatically. "He was at his uncle's funeral. The funeral of a royal family member. Do you know what that means? The entire Royal Court was there. And the second— the *second*— I told him you'd been arrested, he made his excuses and left. Didn't even stay for the reception. It's all over the news and in the gossip magazines! *'Duke's New Romance Calls Him Home.'* It's all anyone is talking about."

Something warm flutters in my chest, but I push it away. "Jack just hates it when someone messes with castle staff," I say, though I'm not sure I believe it myself.

Maggie gives me a look that says she doesn't believe it either. "Does he also give other staff members historic jewelry and take them on dates?" She raises an eyebrow at me. "He genuinely cares about you, Rebecca. I've never seen him like this. He's really serious about you. This relationship could go somewhere."

The idea makes my heart beat faster, but I resist believing it because I feel so bad about losing Luma. What if the Duke and I were on a good path, but I ruined it by losing her? He might not know it now, but if it turns out Luma is gone for good— or worse, injured or killed— Jack will resent me. How could he not? I was the one taking care of Luma when she disappeared.

Joe nudges my hand with his nose, sensing my discomfort. I scratch behind his ears, grateful for the distraction.

Great, I think. *The man falls in love with me and my thank you to him is losing his dog.*

"We have to get Luma back," I say. "I'll never forgive myself if we don't. Jack bonded with that dog immediately and now—"

"We're going to figure out who took her," Maggie says with a confident nod. "We're close, Rebecca."

We reach the grand meeting room, and Maggie pauses with her hand on the ornate doorknob. "Just so you know, the tourism board is in there. I told them they could use our space until theirs is cleaned up, but I also thought, seeing as they're our suspects…"

"It might give us a chance to dig deeper," I grin, nodding at Maggie. "Moments like this and I think we should promote you to *head* Royal Investigator."

"Never," Maggie says. "This is a team effort. Unless the Head Investigator gets extra croissants at breakfast, in which case, I'm sorry, Rebecca, but you've got to move aside and let me take the lead."

I throw my hands up in mock surrender. "I would never stand between a woman and her croissants."

She pushes open the door, and we step into chaos.

Members of the tourism board are scattered around a grand table, surrounded by binders, flyers, and what appears to be a half-assembled three-dimensional heart made of paper. Everyone looks up when we enter, conversations halting mid-sentence.

Matilda smiles at me, throwing her arms open wide. "Rebecca!" She cries, running over and pulling me into a hug. "We heard you were arrested. All of us made statements to Officer Basilier telling her we know you'd *never* vandalize our office, but she just wasn't having it."

"Hmph," Andre says, snorting loudly at the back of the room. He puts a hand on the fake hair that sits on top of his head as if subconsciously avoiding disaster. "Not *all* of us made a statement, actually…"

"We protested, Rebecca!" Pepper says, throwing a fist in the air. She nudges, Lawrence, who's on his cell phone, and he echoes the gesture, albeit with less enthusiasm. "We spoke truth to power."

"Thanks, everyone, really," I say, taking a seat at the table. "How's it all going?"

Matilda sighs, rubbing her temples. "It's a disaster. All our Day of Love plans, ruined. The posters were torn, decorations smashed…"

I notice that the members of the tourism board are sitting side by side, their early disagreements forgotten. Pepper and Lawrence seem to have placed their environmental concerns on hold for a moment, and they're now hovering over decorations. The fights of the past are forgotten— trauma seems to do that to people.

"Any idea who really did vandalize the place, since you all know it wasn't me?" I ask, pulling out a chair and sitting down. Joe settles at my feet, his warm presence reassuring.

"We don't *all* know that," Andre says, shaking his head. "Some of us think you're a *very* suspicious candidate."

"Oh hush, Andre," Matilda scolds him. Then, she adds in a whisper, "We have no idea, but we all think it's connected to the dog that's missing— the one we met? What's her name—"

"The Royal mutt," Andre adds, glancing down at Joe with disdain.

"The dog's name is Luma," I say. "And she means a lot to the Duke."

"Right," Matilda says, leaning forward eagerly, a strained smile on her face. "Is it true? Did he really rush back from his uncle's funeral to help you when you were arrested?"

The sudden intensity in her voice makes me uncomfortable. I notice Maggie giving her a curious look.

"He... came to clear things up," I say carefully. "Since I work for him."

"Dropped everything for you," Matilda presses, her eyes gleaming behind her glasses. "That's what everyone's saying in the village. The Duke left a royal funeral for the dog trainer. How… *romantic*."

Lawrence snorts, finally looking up from his phone. "Who cares? Rich people and their pets."

"I care," Pepper says unexpectedly. "But not because of the Duke. That dog is a living being, and someone took her. It's cruel."

Every time I look at Pepper, I find something new to appreciate. Beside her, Lawrence plays a game on his phone. In contrast to Pepper, I like him less and less every time I see him.

"Exactly," I say. "That's why it's so important we find her."

"Well, while you're playing detective," Andre cuts in with a sniff, "some of us have actual work to do. The Day of Love is in three days, and we've lost all our materials."

Maggie steps in smoothly. "The castle will help in any way we can. We have printing facilities, decorations in storage—"

"That's very generous," Matilda says. "The Duke is always so thoughtful about community events. The Day of Love will be particularly important to him once he sees what we're going to achieve with it. It celebrates Monrovia's ability to form bonds between people. It's about connection. We want to create a magical atmosphere where people can fall in love." She pauses, looking at me. "Unexpected love stories matter, Rebecca. You know that better than anyone, don't you?"

Is she one of these people who doesn't like a commoner dating a Royal? I think, trying to understand what Matilda is getting at.

"Anyway," Matilda continues. "We really need to make sure this day feels magical, for love!"

"And tourism dollars," Lawrence mutters. Then, he adds, "Could you please move that animal? My eyes are starting to water."

Joe hasn't moved an inch, but I recognize someone looking for a fight when I see one.

"Joe, corner," I say quietly. He looks up at me with those soulful eyes, then rises and pads to the far corner of the room, where he settles down with a dramatic sigh.

"That's fine," Andre says, though he doesn't sound particularly grateful.

Matilda stands suddenly, gathering her notes. "We should finalize the schedule. Rebecca, you mentioned before that some of the castle animals might participate in the Day of Love parade?"

"That was before Luma went missing," I remind her. "Now I'm focused on finding her. Given the fact that we've already had one Royal animal disappear, I'm not eager to bring any of our remaining animals into a public space where they could be taken or harmed. Especially considering the person who took Luma could still be out there, waiting to strike again."

"But the Duke," Matilda presses, "will specifically want animals in the parade, won't he? A woman at the rescue told me he adopted all of them at one time, so it *must* be important to him to share wonderful animals with the village..." She gasps, as if she's just had an excellent idea hit her. "What if he had the Duke ride in on the giraffe that lives at the castle?"

"Alfredo?" I say, shocked at the suggestion.

"No, thank you, I'm not hungry—" Matilda squints, confused.

"The giraffe's name is Alfredo," Maggie clarifies helpfully.

"Oh, right," Matilda shrugs as if the giraffe's name is of no importance whatsoever. She holds her hands up in the air like a Director making a movie as she describes the scene in her head. "I'm picturing the Duke riding in on the giraffe, surrounded by heart-shaped confetti falling from overhead. What a photo opportunity!"

"I don't think that's going to work," I start to say. Then, I notice the dejected look on Matilda's face. "We'll see," I say noncommittally. "But I don't think the Duke or Alfredo will be up for it. Depends on whether we find Luma."

"I hope you do," Pepper says, and there's genuine feeling in her voice. "No animal deserves to be taken from their home."

Maggie clears her throat. "Just to clarify, the Duke was really hoping to avoid the spotlight during the community event. Given that his dog is missing and his Uncle just passed away, he'd prefer to fly under the radar." Maggie makes meaningful eye contact with Matilda. "He's already emailed me the request. Please, keep him off the public agenda. He'll attend the event. But as a private citizen."

Matilda nods somberly, placing a careful hand over her heart as if what Maggie has said has moved her deeply. "I understand completely. The good news," she adds, a bright smile crossing her face, "Is that the Duke is back in town and will be able to attend the festival! We'll have so many more visitors if they know a Royal is coming. Even if he's just somewhere in the crowd."

Andre sneezes dramatically. "Can we please focus? Hearts need to be hung, the village square needs decorating, and we need to finalize which vendors get prime spots."

For the next twenty minutes, I sit quietly as they argue over festival details. Joe watches me from his corner, and I can tell he's as ready to leave as I am. My mind keeps drifting to Luma and the strange timing of all these events– the dog's disappearance, my arrest, the vandalism...

Finally, Maggie announces she has another meeting to attend, giving me the perfect excuse to escape.

"I should check on the animals," I say, rising from my chair. Joe is by my side instantly, as if he teleported across the room.

"You'll let us know about the animal parade?" Matilda calls after me. "Even if the Duke can't walk in it, I know the town would love it!"

"I'll see what I can do," I reply, not making any promises. I know full well that I'm not willing to let a single animal walk in a parade until Luma is returned and we've caught the person who took her.

As Joe and I slip out the door, I think about Luma, her face swimming in my mind's eye. I've got a plan to try and track her down. And tonight, I'm going to try it.

I take out my phone to text Jack— he'll want to see this.

———

The afternoon sun casts long shadows across the castle's rescue dog area as I wait for the Duke to arrive. The dogs run around the grass in a pack, smaller dogs chasing big dogs and nipping at their tails. "Be gentle!" I shout as Biscuit, the chocolate lab, catches the nose of a smaller terrier.

Joe sits patiently at my side, his golden coat catching the light as he watches the dogs play. Sometimes, Joe seems more like a human than a dog— like he thinks we're overseeing them together. The other rescue dogs mill about and— as play time winds down— a few of them collapse in a puppy pile, napping in patches of sunlight. I try to enjoy watching the dogs play, but my mind keeps thinking of Luma.

"So you've come up with a new idea to cause trouble?"

The Duke's voice comes from behind me, and I turn to find him approaching with hurried steps.

He looks tired, but there's still a kindness in the way his eyes crinkle.

"I'm not sure of anything anymore," I admit, "but Ace is our best shot. Hawks can cover more ground than any search party. I tried letting Joe track Luma, and he made his way to the cottages, but nothing came of it. Maybe Ace can get an overview."

The Duke nods, coming to stand beside me. Joe greets him with a gentle nudge against his hand, and the Duke absently scratches behind the massive dog's ears.

"I appreciate you trying," he says quietly. "Look at how happy you've made all the rescue dogs while I was away!"

"I'll admit that while it was a great idea to have the castle staff adopt them, I'm not sure anyone is getting quite as much work done."

Myself included, I think without adding the admission aloud.

"Yes, we want everyone working, very important," Jack says in a fake tone that tells me he's not serious at all. "The important thing is the dogs are happy. Luma would have had such a great life here. I can't believe she's gone—"

"I'm not giving up," I say, gently redirecting him to the task at hand. "Let's try the hawk. I've worked with Ace on training exercises, but this will be different. He's never searched for a specific dog before. Still, maybe he can find something."

We walk together toward the aviary, a soaring structure of glass and wrought iron that houses the castle's birds of prey. Ace, the red-tailed hawk, sits regally on his perch, his sharp eyes following our approach.

"What will he need?" the Duke asks.

I reach into my pocket and pull out a bright, blue dog collar. "Something that's connected to Luma. I went to

Benjamin's store and bought the same one she was wearing when she disappeared."

The Duke stares at the dog collar, and for a moment, I think I see his composure crack. But he quickly straightens his shoulders.

"Will it work? Can hawks track by scent?"

"Not by scent," I explain, opening the aviary door. "But they have incredible eyesight. They can be trained to associate finding something and bringing it back with a reward. I've been working with Ace over the past week, teaching him to recognize this collar. If he spots Luma's matching collar there, maybe he'll bring it back or show us where she is."

I approach Ace slowly, speaking in low, soothing tones. He's a magnificent bird, his rust-colored tail catching the sunlight as he shifts on his perch. When I extend my arm, sheathed in a thick protective glove, he steps onto it with dignified precision.

"Good boy," I murmur, bringing him closer to the pouch. "Remember our training? Find Luma, then have a treat."

The hawk tilts his head, his keen eyes fixed on the dog collar. I've done this exercise with him a dozen times in controlled environments, but this is our first real test. My heart pounds with both hope and dread.

The Duke watches intently, his body rigid with tension. "How far can he go?"

"We've only practiced in the castle gardens, but he can fly for miles," I say. "He'll circle the village, the fields beyond, even the forest edge. If Luma is outside anywhere in the area, he should be able to spot her."

I walk Ace outside to the open courtyard, Joe following at a respectful distance. The hawk shifts on my arm, restless and ready.

"Find Luma," I tell him, opening my arm to the sky and showing him the collar one last time. "Retrieve."

With a powerful beat of his wings, Ace launches into the

air. We watch as he circles once, twice, then soars higher, his silhouette growing smaller against the clear blue sky.

"Now we wait," I say, turning to Jack.

He nods, his eyes still fixed on the diminishing form of the hawk. "How long?"

"An hour, maybe two. He knows to come back before sunset."

"I have an idea," the Duke says, grabbing my hand in his. "Follow me." We leave the rescue dogs to play in the menagerie, but Joe follows us into an open castle door. We walk up a set of steps into a turret I've never explored before. There, sits a telescope. "So we can watch where Ace goes," Jack offers.

"Genius," I say, looking into the end of the telescope. I spot Ace, flying toward the edge of the village.

We stand in silence for a moment, both looking skyward. Then the Duke says quietly, "Thank you. For trying everything."

"It's my job," I reply, though we both know I've gone far beyond my job description. "And I love Luma."

"Is that the only reason you care so deeply? There's a hint of a smile in his voice. "Because you love Luma so much?"

There's a quiet moment as I think about this, and then, I answer honestly. "She's not the only one I love," I admit.

The Duke kisses me as if he's been waiting to hear something similar. "I love you, too," he whispers. It's simple. And it's enough.

A wave of relief washes over me as I wrap my arms around him, leaning deeper into his kiss. It occurs to me I've been foolish to think Jack could ever blame me for Luma's disappearance. Still, the ghosts of the past won't let me move on. I think about Travis— my ex-boyfriend— and how quickly he abandoned me after years of companionship simply because he found someone else he liked better. I can't imagine how quickly he would have dumped me if I'd lost his dog.

Don't get ahead of yourself, Rebecca, I think as the Duke runs a hand through my hair. *You might love him, but it doesn't mean this relationship will last.*

As much as I want to relax, the truth is— Jack and I are still getting to know each other.

I bend back to the telescope, watching as Ace makes his way toward the village, taking the same route through the forest that Joe walked only days ago. "He's going toward the cottages!" I exclaim, pointing at the trees. "That's where Joe led me just the other day."

I switch places with Jack. He leans down, looking through the lens of the telescope to verify Ace's flight path. "He's diving!" The Duke shouts in alarm. Quickly, he passes the telescope back to me. I manage to get to the lens just in time to see Ace in a full-out dive, cascading toward the ground with the accuracy of a missile. His wings are folded backward, beak pointed toward the Earth.

"That's a prey dive!" I say, excited. "And he's in the middle of the cottages. He must have found something…"

We watch out the window as Ace heads back toward us, his wings beating the air. Minutes pass by, and before we know it, he's landing effortlessly on the windowsill, holding something in his beak. He drops it into my gloved hand.

It's Luma's collar.

"My word—" the Duke says, reaching out to take the collar. He holds it in his hand, his eyes watering. "It's hers," he confirms, flipping over a metal tag that has Luma's name etched into it.

Suddenly, a horrible thought strikes me. I know the Duke is having the same one, because his eyes look pained. "Rebecca, what if they hurt her—"

"They didn't," I say, shaking my head. My mind searches for the best possible explanation— the one most filled with hope. "They'd have no reason to hurt her. Whoever did this has a motivation, and hurting Luma just doesn't make sense. I think they took the collar off in case we'd put a tracker on her. See?" I whistle at Joe, who walks happily to my side. I unsnap his collar, passing it to Jack. "We got these GPS trackers from Benjamin. Whoever did this might have been in his store before, and they worried we put one on Luma."

"I only wish I had," Jack says, shaking his head.

I reach into my bag— which is filled with pet supplies— pulling out the second GPS tag Benjamin gave me. I clip it onto Luma's collar.

"When you get her back, you will," I say, encouraging. "She'll get this collar back and she'll have a tracker on, so this can never happen again. Ace dove by the cottages. Joe *led* me to the cottages. Luma has to be there, in one of those homes. We'll look tomorrow while everyone is at the Day of Love. We'll wait until it's the middle of the festival, and while everyone is out enjoying the festivities, we'll sneak around the cottages. We're going to find her. She's coming home, Jack."

"What would I do without you?" he says, pulling me close.

I look down at Joe, who's wagging his tail thoughtfully. The three of us stay like that for a moment, all the while feeling the heavy absence of a pack-member… *still missing*.

CHAPTER
Fifteen

DECORATIONS FILL THE VILLAGE SQUARE. Families and couples mill about the central fountain, along with the occasional single villager flying solo. Music echoes in the air, the sound of string instruments setting the town abuzz.

The Day of Love is finally here, and the Duke and I are attending the event in disguise. We both hide under wide-brimmed hats, pretending we're not who we are. Jack keeps his head slightly bowed as we navigate through the crowds at the festival grounds, his hand occasionally brushing against mine in a way that makes my pulse quicken. Joe nips at my heels, and he gets so many stares that I regret not buying him a hat of his own.

"Not sure the hats are keeping eyes away from us," Jack whispers, leaning close enough that I can smell his cologne—it's something subtle and woody that reminds me of the castle library. "And then you factor in Joe—"

Jack glances at Joe, who has stopped to allow a group of children to pet him. They run their hands through his fur and pull at his ears, but Joe takes the intrusion like a champion, assuming the best intentions from all involved. I whistle, calling Joe back to me. The children let out dismayed sounds at his disappearance.

"He's the *real* celebrity here," I reply, adjusting my sunglasses.

"That's true," Jack agrees solemnly. "Here I was thinking *I* might draw too much attention, when all anybody really wants is Joe's autograph."

"They should think twice. He has terrible penmanship."

Jack chuckles, a warm sound that's becoming a familiar jingle in my life. "That's why we keep moving. The key to royal incognito outings is constant motion. And once the crowd reaches its peak, we can sneak away—"

"And look for Luma," I nod. Jack and I have agreed that we'll go to the cottages today and search for Luma while everyone is at the festival. I've brought a pack full of treats and a dog whistle to try to call her. We concluded that most of the villagers would be at the festival within the next hour— giving us time to look around while we wait for the cottages to empty out. "This may require me to break into some cottages and commit a crime," I say seriously. "Can your Royal eyes handle knowing about my criminal activities?"

"I'm afraid I'll have to look away," Jack laughs. "I'm oblig- ated as a Royal to report all crimes I witness, but as a dog- owner— I'll be breaking into those cottages with you if it means getting Luma back."

The Day of Love festival has transformed the Village of Atwood into something straight out of a fairy tale. Red and pink streamers hang between the pastel-colored buildings, and flower petals carpet the cobblestones.

"It's nice to enjoy an event without having to be paraded around," Jack says, stopping to investigate a gelato machine. "Usually they ask me to make some kind of speech or be in a parade."

I cringe, remembering Matilda's request. "There *was* a suggestion that you ride into town on Alfredo's back—"

"They wanted me on a giraffe?" Jack asks, incredulous. "These people have no shame. I'd like to think Alfredo would be equally as horrified at the idea."

"Lucky for you both, Maggie declined all requests on your behalf."

"God bless her," Jack sighs. "This way, I get to see people enjoying themselves and just be a part of the noise. And, of course, be with you." Jack squeezes my hand a little tighter.

We stop at a stand selling heart-shaped pastries. Henri is in charge of the cart, ordering around some of the staff from his bakery. He proudly announces are made with *Le Petit Scone*'s traditional recipe. Jack insists on buying two, passing over money before I can even reach for my wallet.

"Three hundred years of tradition in one bite," he says, handing me a pastry that's still warm from the oven.

I take a bite and nearly groan at the perfect balance of sweetness and spice. "I understand why the recipe hasn't changed in centuries."

We wander further into the festival, stopping at various stands selling everything from handmade jewelry to locally produced honey. Jack seems to know the story behind every tradition, every craft. It's like having a personal tour guide through Monrovian culture, except this guide happens to have royal blood and eyes that crinkle at the corners when he smiles.

"In medieval times, couples would exchange carvings of hawks to express their steadfastness," he explains as we pass a woodworker's booth displaying intricately carved birds. "The hawk was considered a Monrovian symbol of loyalty because they mate for life."

"That's much more romantic than our modern Valentine's Day cards," I say, admiring the craftsmanship.

Jack picks up one of the hawks, turning it over in his hands. "Would you like one?" he asks, something vulnerable lingering in his gaze.

My heart does a little flip. "Are you offering *me* a medieval declaration of loyalty, Your Grace?"

"I'm offering you a beautiful carving," he says with a teasing smile, "but the symbolism isn't entirely lost on me."

Before I can respond, a familiar figure steps directly into our path, causing Jack to nearly collide with her. It's Matilda, her glasses slightly askew as though she's been hurrying.

"Your Grace!" she exclaims, then immediately lowers her voice, darting a glance around us. "I mean... fancy seeing you here." She elbows him as she says the words, trying to imply some kind of joke between the two of them.

"Matilda," Jack acknowledges with a polite nod. To my knowledge, Jack has only met her a couple of times during visits to the tourism board meetings. But he makes an effort to remember everyone's name. I've never once seen him forget a person. "Enjoying the festival?"

"Oh, very much," she replies, adjusting her skirt— today a pleated tartan that reaches well below her knees, paired with a crisp white blouse buttoned to the neck. "It's just lovely to get out of the house for once. I live near the woods, you know, so it's quite a long walk to the square."

I notice her hands are fidgeting with the strap of her sensible leather shoulder bag. She keeps her eyes completely fixated on Jack, ignoring Joe and me entirely.

"Hi, to you too!" I say, waving at Matilda. For the first time, she notices the Duke's companions: an animal trainer, and an enormous fur-ball. Joe tilts his head as if to ask, *"What's wrong with this lady?"*

"Oh! Rebecca and Joe," Matilda says. "Yes. So glad you're — here. It must be wonderful for someone who's not a *true* Monrovian to really get a feel for the culture the Duke and I share."

Not this true Monrovian stuff again, I think to myself, resisting the urge to roll my eyes.

Jack seems to have noticed Matilda's rudeness because he

takes my hand in his and gets ready to take his leave. "Well, it was lovely bumping into you," Jack says smoothly, "but Rebecca and I should keep moving if we want to see everything."

"Of course, Your—" Matilda catches herself again. "Of course. Enjoy your... day." Her eyes dart between us, lingering on me with an expression I can't quite read before she hurries away, disappearing into the crowd.

"That was..."

"Odd," Jack finishes for me. "Perhaps she's excited, being a member of the tourism board? These festivals take much planning as I understand it." We resume our stroll, but the encounter has left a strange feeling in its wake. Jack seems to sense my discomfort and gently takes my hand, his fingers intertwining with mine. "People do act strange around me sometimes, I'm afraid," he says softly. "I hope it's something you think you can get used to. Come on, I want to see the fountain display."

The central fountain in the village square has been transformed for the festival, with floating candles and rose petals drifting across its surface. A local string quartet plays nearby, their music providing a romantic soundtrack as couples gather around the water.

"They say if you toss a coin in on Valentine's Day and make a wish from a heart filled with love, it will come true within the year," Jack explains, fishing two small coins from his pocket and offering one to me. "Monrovian tradition."

"Do you believe it?" I ask, accepting the coin, its metal warm from being in his pocket.

His expression turns thoughtful. "With you here, holding the coin?" He smiles. "I do. It's in powerful hands."

We stand side by side at the fountain's edge, and I close my eyes, clutching the coin. What do I wish for? Something about the man standing next to me, whose world is so different from mine and yet who somehow makes me feel like

I belong in it? Something about this strange new life I've found myself living?

Then, Luma's face appears in my mind's eye. I picture her sweet, big eyes and soft fur, all alone, wanting to find her way home.

I wish that we find Luma today, I think, willing the idea into existence with all of my being.

I toss the coin before I can overthink it, hearing the small splash as it joins hundreds of others at the bottom of the fountain. Jack tosses his a moment later, and when I open my eyes, he's watching me with an intensity that makes my stomach flutter.

"What did you wish for?" he asks.

"If I tell you, it won't come true," I say.

We're standing closer now, and the Duke looks as if he's about to say something when his phone buzzes in his pocket. He gives me an apologetic look before checking it.

"It's from Maggie," he says, frowning slightly as he reads the message. "Apparently, the tourism board is looking for me to make an impromptu speech after all. She says they're waiting at the main stage."

"So much for your day off," I say, trying to hide my disappointment.

"I'm sorry," he says, and he genuinely looks it. "I shouldn't be long. They probably just want a few words of official greeting."

Before I can respond, he leans in and kisses me— not a dramatic, public display, but a soft, quick press of his lips against mine that nonetheless makes my heart race.

"Wait for me?" he asks, pulling back just enough to meet my eyes. "I'll make the speech which— with any luck— will draw quite the crowd. Then we can go to the cottages and look for Luma."

"I'll be here," I promise, and I mean it in ways that surprise even me.

He smiles, gives my hand one last squeeze, and then he's gone, weaving his way through the crowd toward the main stage at the far end of the square. I watch him go, the tall figure in a casual jacket and wide-brimmed hat who, despite his disguise, still moves with the subtle confidence of someone who knows exactly who he is.

I touch my lips, still feeling the warmth of his kiss. I glance down at Joe, wishing deeply that the Duke could find his own furry companion.

———

An hour later, and Jack still hasn't made his speech. Joe and I have waited by the fountain, watching the crowds come and go, but there's been no sound of a microphone crackling. No appearance of the Duke on stage. I'm starting to get that prickly feeling at the base of my neck that usually means something's wrong.

"Let's go look for him, buddy," I say to Joe. He seems to sense my unease, pressing his warm bulk against my leg as we navigate through the increasingly crowded festival. The afternoon sun casts long shadows between the buildings, and I check my phone again— no messages, no calls, no explanation for why a "quick speech" is taking so long.

Joe's ears suddenly perk up, and he turns his head toward a colorful stand selling handmade scarves. Following his gaze, I spot Maggie weaving through the crowd, her blonde braids bouncing as she examines the merchandise.

"Maggie!" I call, waving to catch her attention.

She looks up, her face brightening with recognition as she spots me and Joe. "Rebecca! And Joe, you handsome beast!" She abandons the scarves and makes her way over to us, bending down to scratch behind Joe's ears. "Where's Jack?" She leans in, winking at me. "I said no to all the requests for his involvement today because I thought the two of you might want to enjoy the Festival of Love alone—"

"We *were* alone but—"

"Hey, you can thank me later," Maggie says, throwing her hands in the air. "But I just thought you two needed this time. It's been so hard with Luma missing and the Duke's uncle passing away. I thought… what do they need? Alone time at the most romantic—"

"Maggie!" I interrupt, trying to get her attention. "You just sent the Duke a text message asking him to give a speech. Didn't you?"

Maggie's brow furrows, her hand pausing mid-scratch. "I texted him? About what?"

My stomach drops. "For a speech! About an hour ago. You sent him a message saying the tourism board needed him to make an appearance at the main stage."

"Rebecca, I haven't texted the Duke all day. I've been off-duty since last night— my first proper day off in weeks. That's why I'm here at the festival instead of handling castle business." She pauses, trying to understand. "I purposefully was giving you two some alone time. Do you mean—somebody…"

"Somebody wrote the Duke pretending to be you."

We stare at each other, the implications settling between us like a physical weight. Maggie pulls out her phone, quickly navigating to her messages.

"See?" She turns the screen toward me. "No texts to the Duke today."

My heart rate kicks up a notch. "Then who sent that text?"

"Where did they tell Jack to go?"

"Toward the main stage," I say, pointing across the square. "He said it wouldn't take long but it's been an hour."

Without another word, we both start moving, Joe keeping pace beside us. The crowd seems to thicken as we approach the main stage area, forcing us to weave between groups of people enjoying the festivities, oblivious to our growing anxiety.

The main stage stands decorated with flowers and colorful banners announcing the Day of Love Festival. A local band is currently performing, filling the air with traditional Monrovian music.

Maggie approaches one of the festival organizers, a woman with a clipboard and an official-looking badge. After a brief exchange, she returns to me, her face tight with worry.

"No speeches scheduled for the Duke today," she confirms. "They're actually surprised he's not making an appearance since he usually attends events in an official capacity."

"Someone lured him away," I say, the reality of the situation becoming clearer. "And they used your name to do it."

Maggie is already dialing on her phone. "I'm calling the Royal Guard *and* the Police. If someone is impersonating castle staff to manipulate the Duke's movements, that's a serious security breach." Her breath catches in her throat. "Oh my God, this is all my fault. I cancelled his security today to give you two alone time. He asked me to do it but I should have known it could be dangerous—"

"Maggie, it's not your fault!" I say, just as she puts her phone to her ear.

While Maggie speaks rapidly into her phone, I survey our surroundings with the focused attention I've developed through years of animal training. When working with unpredictable creatures, you learn to notice patterns, behaviors, and environmental changes that others might miss. Now, I apply those same observation skills to the festival grounds.

"Where would someone take him?" I murmur, more to myself than to Joe, though his ears twitch attentively. "They couldn't just drag the Duke through a crowded festival without someone noticing."

A cold sweat rushes through me as I remember what happened in my last romantic relationship. It was so easy for

Travis to leave me. Maybe Jack isn't actually missing. Maybe he's off flirting with other women at the festival. Perhaps with a beautiful visiting supermodel?

Don't be a fool, Rebecca. Jack would never do that, I remind myself. *He would never just forget you and run off. He would talk to you. He has character.*

"Something's very wrong," I say to Maggie, shaking my head.

"I agree," she says, her tone concerned. "What should we do?"

"Joe," I say, kneeling down to my dog's level. "Find Jack."

Joe's training isn't specifically in tracking, but he knows Jack's scent well from our time at the castle. He gives a soft woof of acknowledgment and begins sniffing the ground, his powerful nose working to separate one scent from the thousands surrounding us.

Maggie returns from her call, her expression grave. "Security is on their way."

"There's no time to wait for them. Joe's working on it," I say, nodding toward Joe, who's now moving with purpose toward the east side of the square. "Let's follow him."

Joe leads us away from the main festival area, toward quieter side streets where fewer revelers have ventured. The sounds of music and chatter fade behind us as we turn down a narrow cobblestone alley lined with the backs of shops. Joe's pace quickens, his massive paws moving with surprising grace as his nose remains focused on the ground.

"This makes sense," Maggie says quietly as we follow. "If someone wanted to separate the Duke from the crowd, they'd need a quieter route."

We follow Joe into the outskirts of town, bordering a patch of trees that begins the large expanse of woods running between the village and the castle. Joe keeps his nose to the ground, leading us into the quiet edges of the Village of Atwood. The buildings lose their sheen, clean paint replaced by pastel chips. The streets here aren't as well-maintained, and broken cobblestones shudder under my feet.

"Who would do this?" I ask, though a face has already formed in my mind. As we proceed deeper into the edges of town, the woods seem to take over, trees leaning more urgently over the village. Their leaves seem to offer an answer, taking me back to our conversation with Matilda only hours earlier.

She said she lived near the woods, I think to myself.

Joe stops suddenly, circling an area near a stack of empty crates behind what looks like a storage area for one of the festival booths. He gives a soft whine and paws at something partially hidden beneath one of the crates.

I kneel down and carefully pull it out— a wide-brimmed hat. Jack's hat.

"This is what he was wearing today," I say, my voice barely above a whisper as I hand it to Maggie. "Someone brought him this way."

Maggie takes the hat, her fingers tracing the brim. "Why wouldn't he fight back or call for help? The Duke is no pushover."

"Maybe he didn't realize what was happening until it was too late," I suggest, thinking about how easily someone could approach him— especially someone he knows and trusts. "Or maybe..."

I don't finish the sentence. We both know what "or maybe" might entail— threats, weapons, multiple kidnappers. None of the possibilities are comforting.

Joe whines again, more urgently this time, and continues down the alley. We follow him to where it opens onto a smaller street that runs along the edge of the village, framing the cottages. From here, I can see the beginning of the woods that Matilda mentioned— the woods near her house.

"Maggie," I say, my voice tight. "Earlier today, we ran into Matilda at the festival. She made a point of telling us she lives at the edge of the village, near the woods. And Joe tracked Luma's scent here, to the cottages. Ace found Luma's collar here, too. I think—"

Maggie's eyes widen. "Matilda might have taken Luma? Why?!"

"I don't know, but she's always had this... intensity around Jack. And the way she approached us today felt off, like she was checking to see if I was alone with him."

Joe's sniffing becomes more focused as we approach the tree line. He stops at a spot where the grass is slightly flattened, as though several people recently stood there. Or struggled there.

My stomach twists as I notice something half-hidden in the grass— a button that looks like it came from Jack's jacket. I pick it up, turning it over in my palm. It's distinctive, with a small Royal Crest embossed on its surface.

"He was here," I say, showing Maggie the button. "And I think he was fighting back."

Maggie's already on her phone again, relaying our location to security. Her voice is controlled, but I can hear the tension underlying each word. While she speaks, I scan the ground more carefully, looking for any additional clues.

That's when I notice the footprint leading from a dirt access road toward the trees— fresh tracks that cut through the damp spring soil. Tracks that belong to two sets of shoes.

"Call security again," I say, my mind racing through the possibilities. "Tell them we think Matilda has taken the Duke to her house in the cottages near the woods. Ask them for her address. They have access to records for every citizen, don't they?"

"They do, but Rebecca, we can't just—" Maggie begins, but I cut her off.

"Jack would rescue us," I say. "We can't wait."

Maggie nods, then gets to dialing.

CHAPTER
Sixteen

WE WEAVE through rows of cottages, searching for Matilda's home. Maggie managed to get the address from her sources, and now, we're passing broken-down buildings with thatched rooftops. It's quiet here because everyone is at the Festival, but the silence only adds to the eerie feeling in the air. I glance at one cottage, where a sheet hangs on the window as a curtain. A crumbling retaining wall marks the property's perimeter, sending pieces of old cement tumbling into the yard. The neighbor's house is no better. Next door, an identical cottage features a lawn overgrown with weeds, and an exterior porch railing that tips over, signaling a desperate need for repair. When Joe first brought me here, I was so busy thinking about Luma that I didn't notice the decaying neighborhood.

"The rest of Atwood is so nice," I whisper. "And the word cottage sounds so charming. These houses are—"

"In need of help," Maggie says under her breath. "I know. These cottages are a few hundred years old and nobody's bothered to repair them. They're a long walk to the village center so they're harder to rent. They just— sit here. Unwanted."

We turn a corner and Maggie gasps, pointing at a cottage at the end of the street. "That's it," she whispers urgently. "That's Matilda's house."

Matilda's cottage is a small, rundown structure with peeling paint and a crooked thatched roof. The windows are dark and boarded up with wooden slabs— it's impossible to see inside. The yard is overgrown with weeds and thorny bushes that protect the exterior.

I grip Joe's leash tighter as we approach, my heart hammering against my ribs. Maggie keeps pace beside me, her usual cheerful demeanor replaced by grim determination. The Royal Guard is en route, but the Duke doesn't have time for protocol. Not when he's in there with a woman whose obsession has clearly tipped into dangerous territory.

"How long until the guards arrive?" I ask, keeping my voice barely above a whisper as we crouch behind a row of neatly trimmed hedges.

Sunlight catches in Maggie's blonde braids, turning them golden against the green backdrop. "Ten minutes, maybe more," she answers.

I peer through the foliage at the stone cottage. "We're not waiting."

"But Rebecca—"

"The Duke is in there, possibly injured, definitely in danger. And I'm sure Luma is, too." At the mention of the collie, Joe lets out a soft whine. "If Matilda is desperate enough to kidnap the Duke of Atwood, there's no telling what she might do next."

Maggie nods, squaring her shoulders. "You're right. What's the plan?"

I consider the cottage's layout. One main door facing us, two windows visible from our position, curtains drawn. "Direct approach. I'll take the lead with Joe. If Matilda sees him, she might hesitate."

We move swiftly across the open garden, keeping low. Joe

stays eerily silent beside me, sensing the gravity of the situation. His training kicks in during moments like these, transforming my lovable goofball into a focused working animal.

At the door, I press my ear against the wood. Muffled voices from inside— a woman's voice, high with anxiety, and another sound, a man's groan, weak and disoriented. My stomach tightens. *Jack.*

"Ready?" I whisper to Maggie.

She nods, face pale but determined.

I test the doorknob. Locked, as expected. I step back, position myself, and kick at the door with all my strength. The impact jolts through my arms, but the wood around the lock splinters. Maggie joins me for a second hit, the two of us throwing our combined weights against the door— and it flies open.

Inside, chaos erupts. Joe lunges forward, his massive frame filling the doorway as he lets out a thunderous bark that seems to shake the cottage's foundations. I follow immediately, with Maggie right behind me.

The scene before us freezes time. The Duke of Atwood slumps in an armchair, his head lolling to one side, eyes unfocused but open. His normally immaculate appearance is disheveled, his salt-and-pepper hair mussed, his clothing wrinkled. Across the room, Matilda stands rigid with shock, one arm clutching Luma to her chest, the other holding a small pistol that now swings in our direction.

"Stay right there!" she shrieks, her voice cracking with panic. Luma whimpers, struggling weakly in her grip.

Joe growls, a deep rumble that vibrates through the leash. He wants to run toward Luma, but I hold him steady. One wrong move and this could end badly for everyone.

"Matilda," I say, keeping my voice calm despite the adrenaline coursing through me. "Put the gun down."

"You shouldn't be here," she says, eyes darting between me, Maggie, and Joe. Behind her librarian-like exterior— the neat skirt, the buttoned blouse, the sensible shoes— I can see the desperation of a woman whose carefully constructed fantasy is crumbling. "None of you should be here. This isn't how it was supposed to happen."

"How *was* it supposed to happen, Matilda?" I ask, taking a cautious step forward. "Were you planning to keep the Duke drugged until he fell in love with you?"

Her eyes widen, and I know I've hit the mark.

Beside me, Maggie makes a small, horrified sound. "You're *obsessed* with the Duke?!" she exclaims, putting the puzzle pieces together.

"You don't understand," Matilda says, tightening her grip on Luma. The collie whines again, looking toward the Duke with worried eyes. "*Nobody* understands."

"I think I do," I say, taking another small step. "I understand that you've been in love with the Duke for years. Maybe your whole life."

Matilda's breath catches, and for a moment, the gun wavers.

"You work at the tourism board," I continue, piecing together the fragments of evidence that have been swirling in my mind. "You've watched him from afar, collected every news clipping, and organized events, hoping he would notice you. But he never did, did he?"

"He *would* have," she whispers, eyes flicking to the Duke, who stirs slightly in his chair. "If there hadn't been so many distractions."

"So you created the perfect opportunity," I say, nodding toward Maggie. "The Day of Love Festival. That was your idea, Matilda, wasn't it?"

Maggie's eyes widen. "It *was* her idea. Matilda pitched it at the town council meeting three months ago. Said it would boost tourism during the slow season."

"But it wasn't about tourism," I say, never taking my eyes off Matilda and the gun. "It was about creating the perfect romantic setting. You thought if you could get the Duke there, surrounded by love and romance, he might finally see you."

Matilda's lip trembles. "It would have worked, too, except—"

"Except he wasn't going to be there," I continue. "He had plans to be out of town during the festival, didn't he?"

A tear slides down Matilda's cheek. "He had to leave town for his uncle's funeral. After all the work I'd put in! All the time spent planning. He wasn't even going to *be* here."

The pieces click together in my mind like the tumblers of a lock. "So you kidnapped Luma first. You thought if his beloved dog disappeared, Jack would cancel his trip to come back to search for her."

Joe shifts beside me, sensing my growing tension. I stroke his head briefly, keeping him calm.

"What you didn't count on is that he had *me*," I continue. "Who he trusted to find Luma, even if he couldn't be here himself."

"You were ruining everything," Matilda spits, sudden venom in her voice. "You and your enormous dog, living in the castle, having dinners with him and seducing him into your trap. I watched you. I saw the magazine pictures. I noticed the way he looked at you."

I blink, momentarily thrown. *No one's ever accused me of being a seductress before,* I think to myself. Most of the time, I'm accused of being lazy with my fashion choices and wearing ugly cargo pants. This is a new experience.

I return my attention to Matilda. "So you escalated. You stole my Royal Investigator badge in order to frame me and get me out of the way."

Her smile is small and proud. "From your coat pocket. Remember when I hugged you at the tourism board? You never even noticed. No one ever *does* notice me. They think I'm just some perky middle-aged woman, but I'm more than that."

"You trashed your own workplace and left my badge behind. You knew Officer Basilier had it out for me."

"You deserved it," she hisses. "Coming here, thinking you're so special with your animal expertise and your big dog. The Duke was supposed to come back for Luma and find me. We were supposed to fall in love during the festival. It was a perfect plan!"

"But instead, he came back because of *Rebecca*," Maggie says, her voice steady despite the situation. "Because Rebecca was being framed for something she didn't do. And he loves her."

"Don't say that!" Matilda cries, stamping her foot on the ground. "It's nothing. He's having a fling— it's me he's supposed to be with."

"And when Jack returned," I continue, "you saw another opportunity. You sent him a text message pretending to be Maggie. You told him he was supposed to make a speech. Did you—" I pause, looking at Jack, who appears half-awake. "Did you *drug* him?"

"I offered him a bit of tea before his speech," Matilda smiles. "To clear his throat. It only took a minute to kick in."

"He drank it, obviously," I glance at the Duke, who seems to be becoming more aware, his eyes struggling to focus.

At least Jack gets to be unconscious for this mess, I think to myself, trying to keep my heart rate down. *Whatever she gave him, maybe I should ask for some.*

"It was just something to keep him calm," Matilda says defensively. "I gave it to him by the stage, and then— when he started to feel its effect— told him I'd help him get to a Doctor and led him here before he even understood what was happening. I gave him more to keep him quiet, but it's already wearing off again. Don't worry! He'll be fine. We're going to talk, and he'll understand. He'll see that we're meant to be together."

"That's why you kidnapped him and brought him here," I

say, nodding. "Because you thought if you could just get alone time, you might be able to make him return your feelings.

"Rebecca," Jack says, starting to stir. "What's— what's happening?"

"It's okay, Jack," Matilda says, using his first name with an intimacy that makes my skin crawl. "Everything's going to be fine now. We're together, just like we should be."

The Duke's eyes widen as comprehension dawns. He tries to sit up straighter but seems to lack the coordination. "Did you... drug me?"

"Just temporarily," she assures him, as if that makes it better. "Just until you understand."

Jack's eyes lock on Luma, writhing around in Matilda's arms. "My dog!" He cries out, thrilled to see her. The emotion in his voice makes me realize that Jack's been holding a stiff upper lip since Luma's disappearance. Then, his eyes darken. "You will set her down and let Rebecca and Maggie go. This is between you and me. That's a Royal order." His words come out slurred, and it's clear he's still feeling the drug she gave him. But even in a haze, Jack manages to sound authoritative. It's a skill he's earned through years of practice in diplomacy, negotiating with the leaders of other countries.

"Matilda," I say, agreeing with Jack. "He's right. This has gone too far. Put down the gun, let Luma and Jack go, and we can work this out."

She laughs, high and brittle. "Work *what* out? My arrest? My humiliation? No, there's only one way forward now." She points the gun more deliberately at me. "You need to leave. All of you except Jack. We need time alone."

"That's not going to happen," I say, keeping my voice level despite the fear coiling in my stomach. I don't have a weapon on me that could protect against a bullet.

"It has to!" Her voice rises to a near-scream. "Don't you see? He's *supposed* to be with me! I've studied him for years. I know his favorite books, his favorite foods. I know he prefers quiet evenings to parties, despite what the tabloids say. I know he reads sociology textbooks for fun. I *know* him!"

"Knowing facts about someone isn't the same as *knowing* them," I say gently. "And love doesn't involve kidnapping or drugging someone. Loving someone means being willing to let them go, even if it hurts you. It means giving without expectation, like we do for our pets," I nod at Joe, who's growling by my feet, waiting for me to say the word and allow him to attack. "That's real love."

"What would you know about it?" she sneers. "You're just the animal lady. You probably prefer your dog to people."

She's not wrong there, I think, staring at the deranged woman in front of me. Why do I prefer animals to people? Matilda pointing a gun at me is *Exhibit A.*

"The Royal Guard is on their way, Matilda, along with the Police," Maggie says. "You still have time to do the right thing. Don't make this any worse for yourself."

"She's right," I agree. "This ends now, one way or another. But you get to choose how."

For a moment, uncertainty flickers across Matilda's face. Then her expression hardens. "No. I've waited too long for this chance." She looks directly at me, a terrible clarity in her eyes. "*You're* the problem. *You're* the one he's interested in. If you weren't here—"

"Matilda," the Duke interrupts, his voice stronger now. "Put down the gun. Please."

She looks at him, momentarily distracted, and I consider rushing her. But the gun is too steady, the distance too great. One wrong move and someone gets hurt— the Duke, Luma, Maggie, Joe, or me. I can't risk it.

"Jack, don't you see? I'm doing this for us," Matilda pleads.

"There is no *us,*" he says firmly, though his words still slur slightly. "And there never will be. Not like this. You need help. I can see you get it."

His rejection hits her like a physical blow. She staggers slightly, her grip on Luma loosening enough that the collie manages to squirm free, bolting immediately toward the Duke. As Luma reaches Jack, Joe lets out a soft whine of relief.

But now Matilda has both hands on the gun, and it's pointed squarely at me.

"This is *your* fault," she says, her voice chillingly calm. "If you had just stayed in America with your dog, none of this would have happened."

"Matilda, don't," Maggie pleads. "Think about what you're doing."

But I can see in Matilda's eyes that rational thought left her long ago. Her finger tightens on the trigger, and I feel time slow to a crawl.

In this suspended moment, I think about how absurd it is that after years of working with dangerous predators, I might be taken down by a mousey woman with a crush and a small pistol. I think about Joe, and who will take care of him if something happens to me. I think about the Duke, still not fully recovered from whatever drug Matilda gave him, tied to a chair and unable to intervene.

I meet Matilda's gaze directly. "This won't give you what you want," I say quietly.

"It will give me what I need," she replies, and I see her finger begin to squeeze the trigger.

Joe senses the threat and tenses beside me. Maggie draws in a sharp breath. The Duke struggles to stand, too slow, too unsteady.

And I realize, with perfect clarity, that my brand new life might be about to end. I cringe, as if looking away from my own demise will somehow make it hurt less.

It was a fun ride while it lasted.

CHAPTER
Seventeen

AM I DEAD YET? *Is this what dying feels like?* I think in the darkness that exists behind my closed eyelids. I'm about to open them when I hear a familiar voice calling out from over my shoulder.

"Hands up!"

I turn, facing my rescuer. Officer Basilier stands in the doorway, her service weapon drawn and aimed steadily at Matilda.

I nearly laugh out loud with relief. Officer Basilier— the woman who's been hassling me since I arrived in Monrovia, who thinks I'm a suspicious character— is coming to my rescue.

Never thought I'd actually be happy to see her.

"I said hands up!" Officer Basilier repeats, taking a careful step into the room. She's surprisingly intimidating for someone so petite. Her eyes flick to me briefly, then back to Matilda. "Drop the weapon now!"

Matilda doesn't move. Her gun remains pointed at me, though I can see her hands trembling more violently now.

"You don't understand," Matilda says, her voice rising in pitch as she points at me. "She's ruining everything!" Matilda nods in my direction, her expression communicating that I'm an obvious nuisance.

"I agree," Officer Basilier nods. "Rebecca is the *worst*. To be frank, much like you, I cannot stand Miss Orange. She *absolutely* ruins everything."

"Um, I'm not loving where this is going…" I say.

"However," Officer Basilier glances at me. "She doesn't deserve to die. Not like this. All she did was love a Duke, and poke her nose into an investigation that she was *well advised* to stay out of." She turns back to Matilda. "You're currently committing multiple felonies, and as much as I dislike Miss Orange—"

"Wrong trail again here," I say.

"I am prepared to protect her with my life, because that is the oath I took. Drop the weapon, or I will be forced to shoot. And— I promise you— I'm a faster shot than you are."

But Matilda isn't backing down. Her finger tenses on the trigger, and I realize with cold clarity that she might actually shoot me before Officer Basilier can react.

I need to create a distraction, and suddenly I remember something. During one of our many unpleasant encounters, Officer Basilier had mentioned working with the K-9 unit years ago. Maybe she's open to animal intervention.

It's a long shot, but I have to try.

"Officer B., old buddy," I say carefully, keeping my eyes on Matilda, "I need to know you really have me *covered*."

The emphasis on the last word is deliberate. It's a standard police code word for "be ready to act."

There's a beat of silence, and for a moment I think I've made a terrible mistake.

Then Officer Basilier replies, "Affirmative."

Relief floods through me. She understands.

In one fluid motion, I drop to the floor and shout, "Joe, attack!"

Joe erupts into action, two hundred and fifty pounds of

golden fur launching across the room. He doesn't go for Matilda's throat— he's too well-trained for that— but instead clamps his massive jaws around her calf.

Matilda screams, the gun wavering in her hand as she tries to aim at Joe.

"Luma, fetch it!" Jack shouts from his chair.

I don't have time to wonder what he's doing, because the next moment, Luma springs from her corner like a furry missile. The collie leaps into the air, higher than I would have thought possible, and snaps her jaws around the gun in Matilda's hand.

The weight of the dog and the shock of the bite cause Matilda to release her grip. Luma drops to the ground with the gun in her mouth, tail wagging as if this is the best game ever.

Officer Basilier moves in immediately, kicking the weapon further away when Luma drops it on the floor. Joe maintains his hold on Matilda's leg, ensuring she can't run. Maggie gasps, clapping as she jumps up and down beside me. "Good work, Joe and Luma!" She pumps a fist in the air.

"Release," I command, and Joe immediately lets go, backing up to stand guard. Matilda grimaces when she looks at her leg, letting out a choking sound. Teeth marks scar her calf, blood and deep puncture wounds visible where Joe's bite occurred.

"Andre was right!" She spits at me. "These dogs are a menace!"

"Matilda Jenkins, you are under arrest," Officer Basilier says, pulling Matilda's hands behind her back and clicking handcuffs into place. "You are now being taken into custody. You are advised to speak with a lawyer. The country of Monrovia assures a fair trial by jury of your peers. You have the right to appeal to the sympathy of the Royal Family and ask for a decree of intervention…"

I doubt the Royal Family will be sympathetic to her appeal, I think.

As Officer Basilier continues the Monrovian version of Miranda rights, Maggie comforts both the dogs, while I rush over to Jack and start working on his restraints.

"Are you okay?" I ask, my fingers fumbling with the knots Matilda has tied.

"Splendid," he admits, wincing as I loosen a particularly tight section of rope. "Whatever Matilda gave me is fantastic. We should use it recreationally on the weekends."

I slap his arm for suggesting such a thing. "Are you *really* okay?"

"Fine," he admits. "Just a bit embarrassed that I let a stranger get the drop on me. I underestimated her. That was my fault." Jack rubs his wrists, red marks showing where the ropes had cut into his skin. "Thank you, Rebecca. You were brilliant."

"We were *all* brilliant," I correct him, looking over at Maggie, who's now comforting Luma, stroking the collie's head and murmuring praise. "And what was that 'fetch' command? I didn't know Luma was trained for that."

Jack has the grace to look slightly proud. "I might have taught her a trick or two before I left town. Nothing as extensive as your work with Joe, of course, but the basics. My ultimate intention was to teach her to retrieve books from the shelves of the library. Grabbing a gun never entered my mind, but thankfully she's a smart dog."

"She certainly is," I say, unable to keep the admiration from my voice.

Matilda is sobbing now as Officer Basilier leads her toward the door. "He was supposed to be *mine*! I've loved him my whole life! I studied his favorite books, learned about his interests— Jack! Don't give up on us!"

"I hope she gets help," Jack says, the tiniest bit of empathy in his voice. "For all our sakes."

Officer Basilier hands Matilda off to another officer who's just arrived— I hadn't even noticed the sirens outside— before turning back to us.

"Miss Orange," she says, her voice as stiff as ever. "I'll need your statement about what happened here."

"Of course," I reply. "Thank you for answering Maggie's call."

Despite herself, Officer Basilier's mouth twitches. "I thought you'd need the support. The Royal Guard is notoriously slow. Apparently, though, the Royal Investigators aren't."

"Officer Basilier," Jack says, stepping forward. His posture has changed, reminding me that despite his friendly demeanor, he is, in fact, a Duke. "I believe you owe Miss Orange an apology."

Officer Basilier's eyebrows shoot up. "I'm not much for apologies," she says.

"Then how about we call it even?" I hold out a hand, preparing to shake hers.

"It was good work you did finding the Duke's dog," she admits reluctantly. "And your quick thinking with the code word was... effective."

Coming from Officer Basilier, that's practically a gushing commendation. I decide to take it.

"Thank you," I say.

"In fact," Officer Basilier adds, looking pained at what she's about to say. "I have a few difficult cases in the queue that could use an extra set of eyes. Perhaps the Royal Investigators are interested?"

"We are!" Maggie chirps.

"Most definitely," I add.

"Yes, well," she says, pulling out a notepad. "Let's get those statements now, shall we?"

Maggie steps forward, raising a hand in the air. "I'd like to give my statement first," she says. "This has all been incredibly traumatic and I think talking about it will help me process my feelings. Let's begin the day Luma was stolen…"

"We don't have to start there," Officer Basilier says, annoyed.

Maggie holds a hand up. "Oh yes, we do. You need context. So, I got the call from Rebecca and *ran* to her apartment immediately. It was sunny outside but also sort of cloudy. Actually, maybe it was mainly cloudy. Let me check the weather application on my phone…" Maggie winks at me as she begins going into every detail. She's buying time, hoping to give Jack and me a reprieve.

As Officer Basilier takes Maggie's account of what happened, I cross the room and sit next to Jack, Luma, and Joe, the three of them in a warm pile. Jack pulls Luma into his arms, holding her close.

"It's so good to have the old girl back," he says, patting her stomach.

"I'm sorry I lost Luma in the first place," I tell him, finally confessing a fear that's been bothering me since Luma's disappearance. Thoughts of my last relationship tumble through my mind. That connection taught me that I'm disposable. And, maybe— because of it— I've been afraid that Jack would treat me the same way. "I just felt like I messed up. Like maybe you wouldn't want to be with me anymore."

"None of this was your fault," Jack shakes his head. "You're the only reason she's home!"

"I was worried you'd blame me—"

"Rebecca," he says, leaning toward me. "How could I ever blame you, when I've come to *love* you, so deeply?" He leans in and kisses me, a warm embrace after a cold, terrifying experience. We part, and Joe and Luma bark, the two of them chasing each other in circles around the cottage.

As I look into Jack's eyes, I see something new, there. It's a silent confirmation that I'm safe, etched in the fractal patterns that loop across his irises. The small smile in his eyes tells me

I can count on this connection— whatever it is— to always be here. This is a man who's serious about me. Maggie sees it. Matilda saw it— she saw it so clearly she tried to break us apart. The only person who hasn't trusted in my connection with the Duke…

Is *me*.

"Let's get dinner at *Le Petit Scone?*" I ask. "I'd like to rub it in Henri's face that I solved another case, now that I'm a permanent citizen of Monrovia."

"I'd expect nothing less of you," Jack smiles.

Luma lets out a cheerful yip, and I know exactly how she feels. Luma, and I are both— finally— *home*.

A **WEEK** later and Maggie and I are back in our Royal Investigator office, adding Luma's return to our list of successfully solved cases. At a bed in the corner, Joe lets out a yawn, rolling over lazily.

"This is the best case we've solved so far," Maggie says, grinning as she pins a picture of Luma onto a board we keep to track all of our successfully solved puzzles. The photo of Luma shines next to a picture of the Crown Jewels, which we managed to find after they were stolen by a rogue museum curator. Next to the photo of the Crown Jewels is a copy of the last gossip magazine Rodrigo published before his death, which Maggie and I made sure was avenged. Finally, a photo of Phillipe— the castle's architect— sits in first position. I'll never forget how he was my introduction to Monrovia, and— although it hurts that I never got to know him better— I'm honored to say that Maggie and I solved his murder, bringing the killer to justice. In between the larger photos are smaller Polaroids, outlining minor cases we've solved in between our big victories: a theft at the pet store, a purse stolen in the town square, and graffiti at the fountain.

We stand back and look at our work, arms crossed.

"We're making a difference," I tell Maggie, smiling.

Just then, the bell above the front door clangs. Officer Basilier stands in the threshold, her arms crossed.

"You're about to make a bigger one," she says. "I'm here to collect on my offer."

"Offer?" I ask cheekily. "The word *collect* sounds more like you're calling in a favor."

She steps into our office, sighing heavily as if she'd rather be anywhere else. "It's an offer in the sense I'm giving you the *grand opportunity* to assist the Monrovian Police. You can learn from us and," she swallows as if the words taste bad in her mouth. "We would *appreciate* the extra help from the Royal Investigators."

My heart pounds in my chest. If Officer Basilier is asking for our help, the case must be a big one.

"May I?" Officer Basilier says, motioning at a set of chairs in the corner. "Join me. You're going to want to sit for this one."

———

Keep reading for an excerpt from "A Perilous Proposal," Book Five in the Rebecca Orange Castle Cozy Mystery Series!

A Perilous Proposal

We've done so much good, I think proudly, stepping back to admire our latest masterpiece: the ever-glorious Investigation Board. Maggie and I update it religiously, pinning up case photos like it's a very dramatic scrapbook. Today, our center-piece is a glossy close-up of Mr. Plumfeathers— an exotic African Grey parrot who recently disappeared and triggered a three-day, village-wide bird-hunt that involved a bell tower, one scandalized neighbor, and a lot of squawking. He's now proudly perched in our "Solved" section, looking both colorful and smug. Officer Basilier asked for our help finding the parrot because we did such a good job locating the Duke's lost Collie— although I've yet to receive any thanks from her.

"I'm not going to lie... I was hoping Officer Basilier was giving us a bigger case than a missing bird," I say, adjusting the red thumbtack like it's the finishing jewel in a royal crown. "But I'm glad Mr. Plumfeathers made it home. Another triumph for the two greatest detectives in Monrovia!"

Maggie looks up from where she's nursing her thumb, now wrapped in a tiny bandage that somehow still coordinates with her outfit. When we'd finally cornered Mr. Plumfeathers in the bell tower, she reached for him before I could yell *"parrots bite!"* Which, to be fair, is common knowledge. That beak could crack walnuts, and apparently, thumbs.

"I'm not sure I'd call being mauled by a parrot a 'triumph,'" she deadpans.

"He didn't mean it," I protest. "He's a bird with the emotional intelligence of a toddler and the jaw strength of a bench vise."

Maggie raises an eyebrow. "That bird knew *exactly* what he was doing. I'm just saying, if a fryer happened to be nearby, fried parrot probably tastes exactly like chicken…"

"Pretending I didn't hear that," I sing, loudly and cheerfully, backing away from both the investigation board and the mental image of deep-fried parrot.

Our office—the Royal Investigators Headquarters—isn't large, but it's ours. A few months ago, it was just a sad little storefront in Atwood with cracked linoleum and suspicious wallpaper. Then Maggie worked her signature magic: sweet-talked the castle staff, charmed the elderly landlord (who now leaves her suspiciously poetic rent notices), and transformed the space into something between a detective agency and a Pinterest board.

Up front are our mismatched desks—hers a vision of organization, mine resembling a slow-moving paper avalanche. We have a couple of cozy chairs for clients, an always-full candy jar (bribery works), and of course, the Investigation Board—a corkboard-turned-conspiracy-map with color-coded string and Maggie's sharp cursive narrating the madness. Out back is our "interrogation lounge," which is really just a fancy name for a room with a table, a kettle, and occasionally, a cat. And nestled beside my desk, sprawling across a custom dog bed the size of a twin mattress, is Joe—my Tibetan Mastiff and co-investigator. Currently, he's snoring like a freight train with fur.

"Speaking of Plumfeathers," Maggie says with a grin, "I

did enjoy watching Officer Basilier choke on her pride. I think we've moved from 'tolerated nuisances' to... whatever comes just before 'acquaintances.'"

"I'm not convinced," I say, picturing Basilier's forced smile when she begrudgingly asked for our help. "She tolerates us the way one tolerates socks that slide down into your shoes— only when absolutely necessary."

Joe sighs in agreement from across the room, one giant paw twitching in his sleep like he's dreaming of justice. Or meatballs.

"She did apologize, though," Maggie points out, twirling in her chair like an unusually elegant five-year-old. "That's something."

"True," I admit. "Although I was hoping her exact words word be, 'Sorry, Rebecca, for arresting you and trying to ruin your life.' But I guess we've all grown. Last year, she would've either taken credit for the find or filed a noise complaint against the parrot. Or me. Maybe both."

"No," Maggie says, laughing, "she would've *blamed you* for kidnapping the bird. And honestly, you do have a suspicious face."

She spins one more time and then pauses, looking suspiciously thoughtful. That's Maggie's tell—when she stares at the ceiling like it holds all her secrets.

"Maggie," I say, squinting. "What did you do?"

"It's not *what I did*," she replies, all innocence and dimples. "It's what *we're doing*."

"I'm so alarmed. Go on."

"Well… you said you enjoyed working with Basilier—"

"*Once*," I clarify, raising a hand. "Enjoyed in the same way you might enjoy jury duty if they give you donuts. It doesn't mean I want to make a habit of it."

Maggie leans forward, practically vibrating with suppressed glee. "But what if I told you she asked for our help again? *Real* help. No birds. No claws. A good old-fashioned crime. Like... with destroyed property and motives and everything!"

I stare at her. My heart flutters, just a little. Officer Basilier asking us for help on a *legit* case? Not because I'm an animal trainer or because Maggie is irresistible to landlords, but because we're... good? Because we're the real deal?

"Is this a fantasy scenario, or did you already agree to something on my behalf?"

Maggie checks her watch, which is her way of saying "yes" without actually saying it. "We're meeting her at Café de Flore in an hour."

Of course we are.

Across the room, Joe lifts his head, blinking blearily at us like he's sensing the shift in tone. Or possibly just the word *café*.

"What do you think, Joe?" I ask. "Ready to work with our least favorite Police Officer again?"

Joe gets up, stretches with a groan, and saunters over to the door like a dog who knows his destiny is wrapped in croissants and chaos.

And just like that, the game is afoot.

———

To keep reading, order "A Perilous Proposal" in paperback today!

Dear Reader,

Thank you for dedicating your time to the world of Monrovia and Rebecca Orange! These books mean so much to me, and my hope is always that what I've written gives you the chance to escape to a cozy new place.

I love hearing from readers (seriously, it makes the job so fun!). Please reach out to me anytime by visiting www.valeriebrandy.com or finding me on social media, even if it's just to say "hi" or talk about flower names for coffee. Monrovia is special because of the community there, and I love forming the same cozy friendships around my books.

You can also join my author club mailing list for free give-aways and updates on new releases. Scan the QR Code below or visit my website to join!

Warmly,

— Valerie Brandy

www.ingramcontent.com/pod-product-compliance
Lightning Source LLC
Chambersburg PA
CBHW061519050726

47593CB00002B/652